"DON'T BE SMART WITH ME, LASSITER. YOU TELL ME WHO THAT WAS AT THE WINDOW, OR I'LL COME IN THAT CELL AND GET IT OUT OF YOU."

Marshal Lund felt confident with a number of the townsmen and local cowhands behind him. He was going to show everyone who was boss.

"Come on in, Lund," Lassiter challenged. "I would welcome that, and I'd treat you real special."

Lund was held silent a moment by the icy tone of Lassiter's voice. But he had dealt the hand and now he was going to have to play the cards.

The marshal turned to one of the men. "Hold this lantern. And shoot him if he tries to escape. I'm going to teach him a lesson."

Lund turned the key in the cell-door lock, pulled the iron-barred door back and came toward Lassiter, his pistol raised. As he neared Lassiter, he brought the pistol down in an arc.

Lassiter had no trouble blocking Lund's forward motion. With his free hand, he landed a heavy blow with his fist into Lund's midsection, doubling him over. Then Lassiter pulled him up by the hair and landed a savage blow to his face, knocking him backwards, through the cell door.

There was a roar of gunfire and Lassiter moved instantly to one side . . .

Books by Loren Zane Grey

Lassiter
Ambush for Lassiter
Lassiter Gold
Lassiter Tough
The Lassiter Luck
A Grave for Lassiter
Lassiter's Ride
Lassiter on the Texas Trail
Lassiter and the Great Horse Race

Published by POCKET BOOKS

LOREN ZANE GREY

LASSITER AND THE GREAT HORSE RACE

POCKET BOOKS

New York   London   Toronto   Sydney   Tokyo

This book is for John, Laura, and David.

With many thanks to: Kathleen Bradley, Andrea Cirillo, Ruel Fischmann, and Judy Lamppu.

An *Original* Publication of POCKET BOOKS

POCKET BOOKS, a division of Simon & Schuster Inc.
1230 Avenue of the Americas, New York, NY 10020

ISBN: 0-671-63895-5

First Pocket Books printing May 1989

10 9 8 7 6 5 4 3 2 1

POCKET and colophon are trademarks of Simon & Schuster Inc.

Printed in the U.S.A.

1

THE SUN PAUSED OVERHEAD, bringing midday heat to the rocky foothills below. Lassiter had been crossing the stretch of sagebrush and rock for the better part of the day, awaiting his chance to find shade and rest his horse.

Lassiter was no stranger to hard riding and severe conditions. But there seemed to be no letup to the strong sun this day. He rode down out of the foothills, his big black stallion picking the easy trails toward the bottom. Summer had brought intense heat to Wyoming Territory, and Lassiter was hoping to find a cool place to spend the afternoon once he reached Cheyenne.

There was still a full two weeks time before the Great Horse Race, the Fourth of July event that had brought Lassiter into the territory. A long time friend who had a cattle spread, Jack Stanford, had invited Lassiter to represent his Double 7 Ranch in the race. Each ranch was to ante a thousand dollars in gold for the event—winner take all, and Lassiter would ride his big black stallion across the twisting miles of rugged mountain-and-foothill country for the Double 7. If he won the race, it would mean big money for himself and Jack Stanford.

But there would certainly be a good many more riders with the same idea. Since this horse race was billed at such high stakes, Lassiter was certain it would bring any number of the rough breed in from all over. The race would be a tough one.

Lassiter removed his hat and wiped his brow with a forearm. Layers of thick dust had settled into his black clothes, coloring them almost a dull gray. In this kind of weather a man should think twice about being out of doors for very long, much less riding over miles of sunbaked back country. It was enough to make Lassiter wonder if he was a bit sun-dozed already.

He crossed a small bottom and sat his stallion atop a ridge. Through the shimmering heat, Lassiter judged Cheyenne to be less than a three-mile ride. But he knew that merely reaching the town would just be the beginning to finding his way to the Double 7 Ranch. He couldn't be sure who did and who didn't like his friend Jack Stanford, and who might not want a stranger riding a stallion that looked to be fast.

Cheyenne was a tough town, born of the Texas trail herds and a hardened railroad. With its settlement, the elbowing for land and power had begun in earnest. The strongest would hold up and the others would have to move on. And Lassiter knew for certain that Jack Stanford was among the strongest. He knew how much Jack Stanford could take, and knew just how much he could dish out, as well.

Just after the Civil War, Lassiter had been working a cattle spread in the Texas panhandle with Stanford

6

and had watched him take on two hardened gunmen who wanted to crown him with their fists. Stanford had put them both down, then one of them had gotten a bullet into his left side before Stanford could empty his pistol into both of them. Lassiter had taken Stanford to Abilene to find a doctor, and at Stanford's insistence, they had ridden for three days without stopping. By the time they reached Abilene, Stanford was out in the saddle—but still alive.

Now, Lassiter rode off the ridge and back onto the trail toward Cheyenne. After stopping at a small creek to water his horse and drink his fill himself, he brushed the dust from his clothes and prepared for the rest of the ride to Cheyenne.

As he was prone to do before he rode into a strange town, Lassiter checked his two black-handled Colt revolvers, as well as his Winchester rifle. Black leather and pistols were his trademark, and there was a lot of men who wanted to call themselves better than the gunfighter dressed in black. He then climbed back into the saddle.

Overhead, cries from a red-tailed hawk pierced the still air as it circled the rocky hills and gullies. Lassiter was about to ride again when he spotted someone on horseback riding in a gully just out from where he was sitting his own stallion. The horse was a large blood bay, sleek and quick of foot. Its rider knew the horse well and how to put it through the paces.

It seemed to Lassiter that the rider had to be crazy. Nobody would normally be running a horse in heat like this. But despite the heat, the horse seemed to be running smoothly.

Lassiter continued to sit his stallion and watch. The rider, finally noticing him, slowed the bay to a trot. He turned and rode toward Lassiter, approaching cautiously, waving his hat to show he was friendly.

Lassiter nodded, his arm resting lightly on the pommel of his saddle. He could see the rider was likely a local cowhand, not much more than twenty years of age. He was certainly riding a fine horse, one that was no doubt scheduled to be entered in the race. The rider brought his bay to a stop, the horse breathing heavily. There was an air of confidence about him that Lassiter could not fail to notice.

"You're a stranger in these parts," the cowhand said, eyeing both Lassiter and his black stallion. "Good horse you've got there."

Lassiter nodded. "That bay doesn't look so bad, either."

The cowhand smiled, his confidence showing even more. Lassiter didn't think the man meant any harm—just curious. But he didn't want to take anything for granted. As long as the two of them stuck to discussing horses, they could remain on familiar ground.

"Would you be looking to enter that black stallion of yours in the upcoming race?" the cowhand asked.

"It's possible," Lassiter answered. "What about you and that bay you're riding?"

"I'm going to win the race on the back of this horse," the cowhand said bluntly. "No question about it."

The cowhand still sounded confident, but Lassiter watched his eyes as they looked over every inch of his black stallion. Until now, the cowhand had been sure he would win the race. Now he was wondering.

"I guess time will tell," Lassiter said.

"Who you riding for?" the cowhand asked. "I'm riding for the Box Y."

"I'm riding for Jack Stanford's Double 7 spread,"

Lassiter said. "You wouldn't happen to know that brand?"

"Yeah, I do, matter of fact," the hand replied. "You a friend of Jack's?"

"An old friend," Lassiter answered with a nod.

"Jack's a tough one," the cowhand remarked. "He don't bow down to nobody."

"That's the Jack Stanford I know," Lassiter said, nodding again. "I guess I'm in the right territory."

The cowhand studied Lassiter for a time longer, then said, "You ain't dressed like most cowhands I've known. You're dressed like a gunman. You ride a mighty fine horse, but I'd say your aim was to do dirty work."

"That's a hard way to talk to someone you've just met," Lassiter remarked. "You don't even know me."

"I know your kind," the hand said, twisting his face into a frown. "It don't seem to me like Jack Stanford would have your kind around."

"I came to race," Lassiter told the hand firmly. "I don't use my guns unless I have to."

"I wouldn't figure Jack to even enter the race," the hand said bluntly. "I don't think he could scrape together even half the entry fee."

The remark left Lassiter stunned. He hadn't been up in this country to see his friend since their days together in Texas, but he was certain Jack Stanford wasn't poor. No matter the situation, Jack always seemed to come up with what it took to look good.

Lassiter was going to ask the cowhand what he meant by the remark when he heard the crack of rifle fire, then saw the cowhand jerk in the saddle as a bullet thumped into his back. The cowhand's face took on a strained expression before the light in his eyes faded and he tumbled sideways off the blood bay.

Lassiter was already down off his black, his Winchester in hand, as another shot sounded and a bullet whined off a rock just behind him. He let his stallion gallop away, with another slug zipping through the sagebrush just beside him as he took cover.

Crouched behind a rock, it was at first hard to see where the shooting was coming from. But soon Lassiter had pinpointed a cluster of juniper trees growing partway up the hill just opposite the creek.

He waited for another shot to be fired, then aimed his rifle. After three quick shots he rushed from his position to get closer to the junipers. He saw flashes of someone running from the junipers, up and over the top of the hill, and knelt to get off a shot. But the bushwhacker was too close to the top.

Lassiter knew his best chance now was to get to his black stallion and give chase. After retrieving the horse, he rode up the draw on the left side of the hill. He was hoping to find the bushwhacker coming across, traveling away from town. But the bushwhacker had taken the opposite direction to make his escape, and Lassiter could only watch as a thin plume of dust rose in the distance, through the foothills that reached toward the mountains to the south.

Lassiter rode up into the junipers and dismounted. He found a number of shell casings. They were from a .44–40 Winchester—a common rifle. The bullets were interchangeable with a .44-caliber pistol. In fact, it was the same type of rifle he used.

After looking around further, Lassiter could see no traces of blood or anything else that might show he had wounded the bushwhacker. He mounted again, wondering if the killing had something to do with the upcoming horse race. The odds were better than even that it did. Anyone who was as good a rider as the dead cowhand had been—riding a horse as good as the blood bay—would certainly have to be considered a favorite in the race.

The more he thought about it, the more Lassiter was certain the shooting had to do with the race. There was going to be a lot of money at stake, and getting rid of one good rider could open up the gates for someone else.

But now Lassiter was in the middle of it. The shooting had been planned, that seemed certain. But the bushwhacker certainly hadn't expected him to be there.

Lassiter turned his stallion and rode back down to where the cowhand was lying on his stomach. Blood had collected in a small pool in the dust just under his right side. But it was just a small pool. He had died almost instantly, and his heart had quit before much blood could pump out of him.

The air was still hot, and the flies were beginning to find the dead hand. Lassiter wondered what he should do. He couldn't just leave the man lying in the dust, but he didn't want to make anybody suspicious of him, either.

After thinking awhile, he decided his best move was to take the body into Cheyenne and just tell what had happened. A killer doesn't take the body into town. Also, someone in town might know who would have cause to murder this cowhand in cold blood.

Lassiter caught the hand's blood bay and was just getting ready to lift the body over the saddle when he heard a group of riders approaching in a hurry. In no time there were five men reining in their horses through thick clouds of dust. They all had rifles out, trained on Lassiter. All were looking at the body.

"It's Allen Hutton," one of the riders said, a small

and wiry hand with thick blond hair. He jumped down off his horse and rushed to the fallen cowhand. "He's stone dead," he told the others, looking up at Lassiter.

"Johnny, you sure he's dead?" one of the other riders asked. He looked short and thick in the saddle, his hair and clothes slick with sweat.

"I'm sure," the small one named Johnny said.

Lassiter shook his head. "I didn't kill him."

"Put your hands up where we can see them, mister," the short, heavyset one ordered. He held his rifle steady. "A man can't get away with cold-blooded murder in this country, stranger."

Lassiter raised his hands. His worst fears had come to pass; now, besides being a stranger, he was considered a killer to boot. Things were going to be harder than he had ever imagined.

2

THE YOUNG COWHAND NAMED JOHNNY stared hard at Lassiter. He seemed frightened and in awe at the same time, as if he knew he was looking at an honest-to-goodness gunfighter and believing for certain how deadly he was. Lassiter could see that he was hardly twenty years old, and impressionable. He wasn't like the other cowhands, who no doubt had come up the trail with Texas herds and seen death a number of times apiece.

The heavyset one continued to keep his rifle trained on Lassiter. He was now telling the others how lucky he had been to be in the area when the shooting took place, so he could find them and catch this stranger quickly.

Lassiter frowned. He couldn't remember anyone being around when the shots were fired—except the bushwhacker in the junipers along the hill. He would have seen anyone else, or at least noticed the dust from a horse.

The heavyset one was still staring at Lassiter. He grinned. "You shouldn't come into new country and shoot somebody, stranger. That ain't good for your health."

"It's a good thing you found us quick, Hardy," the young one named Johnny finally spoke up. "Otherwise, he might have got away."

"Malone, here, deserves to get credit from the marshal," another of the cowhands put in. "I don't see him out here. Where's he at when we need him?"

"We don't need him when we've got Hardy," Johnny said.

Hardy Malone. The heavyset hand's name seemed to ring a bell deep in Lassiter's mind. But it was so deep that Lassiter couldn't place where he had heard the name before. He hoped it would come to him, but right now his major concern was to get out of this situation.

"Yeah, I guess I was pretty lucky," Malone said, staring at Lassiter through a thin smile. "I came as quick as I could. Good thing I found you boys."

"Just one thing, I didn't kill this man," Lassiter protested.

"Yeah, you killed him," Malone said quickly. He used his forearm to wipe sweat from his brow.

"No, I didn't," Lassiter said. "I wouldn't be here now if I had. I would have ridden right off."

"That's what they all say," one of the other men put in. "We just got back here before you could get away."

Lassiter looked from man to man and finally back to Hardy Malone, who was pushing this whole thing harder than anyone else. It occurred to Lassiter that though Malone might be a working cowhand, of sorts, his eyes and mannerisms suggested he was more likely a hired gun.

Lassiter worked again to remember where he had heard Malone's name before. But it still wouldn't come. A few questions of Malone, he thought, might bring some answers.

"You must know everybody in this valley," Lassiter said to him. "Did you come up with one of the first trail herds?"

"Hardy ain't been here but a month," the hand named Johnny quickly spoke up. "He came to work for our outfit, Trace McCord's Box Y."

"Shut up, Johnny," Malone blurted. "It ain't none of his business who I am and where I come from."

"What are you trying to hide, Malone?" Lassiter asked quickly.

Malone fumed with anger. "Just back away from the horse and the body," he ordered. "I ought to just pull the trigger here and now."

"Yeah, stranger," the little one named Johnny put in. "After what you did, you don't deserve to live."

Lassiter knew from the way they were all acting that nobody would likely stop Malone from killing him if he took the notion. What seemed odd was the fact that everyone seemed to trust Malone so much, even though he hadn't been in the territory for more than a month.

Hoping Malone might not act too hastily, Lassiter kept his hands raised and backed away from the body. He tried again to convince the riders of his innocence.

"I'm telling you, I didn't kill this man. Someone shot him in the back while I was talking to him."

"Don't tell me that," Malone said. "I *saw* you shoot him."

Now Lassiter understood. Hardy Malone had to be

the man who had killed the cowhand—the bushwhacker on the hill—shooting from among the trees. There had certainly been no one else around but that bushwhacker, and he had managed to ride away.

After killing Allen Hutton, Lassiter reasoned, Malone knew he had to find somebody immediately who would go with him to find the body. That there was someone with Hutton could work to Malone's advantage, because the stranger could be accused of the killing.

It was a good way for Malone to free himself—pin it on someone else, a stranger nobody knew or cared about. And even better, a stranger who was a gunfighter. It all seemed to fit. Malone was certainly sweaty enough to have ridden hard in the heat. The others were hot but not drenched like this man. And he seemed very defensive about what he was doing in the territory.

"This stranger is real trouble," Malone then told the others. "He would likely have taken that blood bay for his own, on top of it all. I don't think we ought to wait any longer. I say we string him up."

The suggestion to quickly hang Lassiter caused some of the hands to think twice. The young one named Johnny had been talking as if he saw Malone as some kind of hero. But now he was frowning, and finally he spoke up.

"Maybe we'd just ought to take him to town," he suggested. "Maybe we shouldn't hang him. Let the law decide."

Malone looked down at him from his saddle. "The law ain't going to help us," he told Johnny in a gruff tone. "That marshal will just put this stranger in jail, and before you know it, he'll find some way to get off."

"Just the same, we ain't supposed to decide for the law," Johnny pointed out.

"You figure justice will get done if we turn him over to the marshal?" Malone asked with an even sharper edge to his voice. "He ain't been able to convict anyone yet."

"He ain't supposed to convict people," Johnny said. "He's just supposed to see that the law is carried out. Judges are for deciding who's guilty, judges and juries."

"What's all this proper title stuff?" Malone asked. He pointed to Lassiter. "This stranger is as guilty as guilty can be. And anyone who don't have the guts to do what's right ain't much of a man."

Johnny was looking at Malone as if he had lost a good friend. "It ain't a matter of being a man or not," Johnny finally said. "It's a matter of being a fool. Suppose he's innocent?"

Lassiter could see that Malone was getting angrier by the second and now considered Johnny a real thorn in his side.

"You just stay out of the way while the rest of us do what's supposed to be done," Malone finally told the young cowhand.

Another cowhand then spoke up: "Johnny's right. We're acting too fast here. We ought to take him into town. Frank Lund can get the circuit judge in. If he's guilty, he'll hang."

"No! We ought to do it now," Malone said again.

"We ain't the law, Malone," Johnny said. "And that's a fact."

Quickly, one of the other hands then spoke up in Malone's favor. "No, Johnny, you don't know how it works. The law's too soft. Takes too long. Hardy's right. String him up now, before something happens that he gets off."

There was discussion back and forth among the men about it. The discussion turned to arguing. Finally, Johnny and the other cowhand who had argued against the lynching rode off toward Cheyenne. Lassiter knew they were headed to find the marshal, and he watched them disappear into the distance, a high column of dust rising behind them.

Then Malone and the other three dismounted and surrounded Lassiter, Malone in front.

"We've got a rope that's going to fit you just right," he said. "Just right."

Lassiter looked into the distance once again, hoping that Cheyenne wasn't that far away. He certainly didn't have much time now.

Johnny Ridge, the young, blond cowhand who had decided it wasn't right to lynch someone without a fair trail, rode hard with the other cowhand toward Cheyenne. They hoped to reach Frank Lund's office before it was too late.

Though he couldn't quite decide what it was, something had struck Johnny Ridge about Hardy Malone wanting to hang the stranger so quickly. Though he didn't know Malone to speak of, Malone had always seemed like someone who had a mind of his own, someone to look up to.

But today had proved to Johnny Ridge that Hardy Malone really wasn't the kind of person he would have people think he was. Malone was in favor of killing the stranger without blinking an eye, and Johnny felt it wasn't good to just hang a man without thinking hard about it first.

Johnny had been in the territory just under two

months. He had drifted in after the winter, looking for a job. Most hands hadn't been here long, though some had been around for nearly two years. They had come north with Texas trail herds and settled with one of the outfits, riding the roundups to help brand and drive the cattle to market at the railheads.

The Box Y ranch was one of the biggest operations in the valley. Johnny liked working for the Box Y, and he liked Trace McCord, the owner. What's more, McCord had a daughter named Clara, whom everyone considered something special. A picture if there ever was one . . .

Malone had drifted in a little after Johnny Ridge had, for the spring roundup. The older man had been spending his time in the local saloons, talking of hiring on with an outfit but never really looking too hard for work.

Malone had gotten on most everyone's good side one afternoon when he had run two drifters out of town who had started trouble in one of the saloons. Frank Lund had been out of town, and Malone had stopped a shooting. It was something he had taken a lot of credit for.

After that, there were those who were speculating that Malone would likely get an offer to ride in the horse race for somebody. Everyone was talking about the race, and everyone knew that Allen Hutton was going to ride for the Box Y and likely win the race. Somebody like Hardy Malone, on a good horse, could change all that.

As the time drew ever closer to the race, Malone still hadn't said if he was riding for anyone or not. But he continued to hang out in the saloons and make himself popular, and also get on the good side of Frank Lund, who felt he owed Malone something for helping when he was out of town. Had the two drifters shot somebody, Lund knew he would have been blamed for not being around to do his job.

So, early that morning when Malone had come riding into the Box Y ranch yard as fast as he could, yelling that a stranger had shot Allen Hutton in Porter Draw, everyone had believed him. They had ridden quickly, wanting to catch the killer before he got away. But no one had really expected Malone to insist that they hang him right then and there.

No one knew this stranger dressed in black at all. Johnny seemed to think that despite the fact they had found him next to the body, they shouldn't decide for themselves that he had killed Hutton. If he had, it would at least be worth knowing the reason why before they hanged him.

Johnny was even more intent now that they keep the stranger from being lynched. He and the other hand rode into Cheyenne and didn't slow their horses until they got to the marshall's office. There were already people out in the streets, wondering why they were riding recklessly through town. And the marshal, Frank Lund, was already out in front of his office.

"What the hell is your hurry?" Lund asked.

"Hardy Malone and some of the Box Y hands are fixing to lynch a stranger in Porter Draw," Johnny replied. "They claim he killed Allen Hutton."

"What?" Lund said.

"Allen Hutton's been shot," Johnny explained. "Hardy Malone says he saw this stranger do it, a man all dressed in black. Hardy and the others are going to string him up."

"Who's the stranger?" Lund asked.

Johnny shrugged. "I don't know, but we'd better hurry, or they'll hang him for sure."

The more Lund thought about it, the more he thought he should know who this stranger in black was. More out of curiosity than a sense of duty, Frank Lund hurriedly unhitched his horse, gathered two deputies, and led them all at full gallop toward Porter Draw. It had been some time since a stranger had caused this kind of stir in the valley.

3

FRANK LUND WAS MIDDLE-AGED and not much more than a drifter himself. In his younger years he had been with various groups of border raiders in southern Texas. It was there he had learned to use a gun and kill whenever the mood struck him. He had then served in the Confederacy, and had turned to punching cattle after the war.

Becoming a lawman was the last thing Frank Lund had ever thought about doing, until he realized it was that or squander himself away punching cattle. He was smart enough to realize that raiding was not a smart way to make a living—sooner or later someone was going to kill you—and so he had decided to leave his past behind him and start over.

After a time he began to see that a lot of men on the wrong side of the law turned to wearing a badge and profiting from it. Being a marshal had its drawbacks, but in the right town, he could see that it was an easy road to retirement—if he played his cards right.

Lund had learned the art of keeping the peace for profit by careful observance. He had been a deputy in some of the Kansas cowtowns before moving north. Abilene, particularly, had taught him a lot about how to run a town.

As a deputy, Lund had learned how to be smart and get to know the right people, so he could protect the interests of those who could keep him in office, those who could benefit him the most. If they didn't have money and weren't respected in the community, Frank Lund wasn't interested in them.

Lund had brought this philosophy to Cheyenne two years before, and had come to profit from it. He knew who to please and who to ignore. His job was secure. Most folks respected him, whether they liked him or not. Being liked was something he could take or leave, since he wasn't really keeping the peace to gain friends among the common folk; it was the people in power he was careful to please. And the common folk just stayed out of his way. Having the power of a tin badge on his side was something he felt real comfortable with.

And on top of it, Lund was also capable. Though he wasn't the type who struck fear into someone, he was deceptive. He didn't look as if he could pull a pistol in a hurry, but he could. And he had already killed three men to prove it.

Now, as he rode toward Porter Draw with the two Box Y hands and the two deputies, Lund thought again of the stranger dressed in black. Something was stirring within his memory, something he remembered in Abilene when he had been a deputy there.

A stranger dressed in black had been jumped by three gamblers, and the three had lost their lives because of it. Lund had come in to take the stranger in, but the stranger had never gone to jail.

Witnesses had taken Lund aside and told him that the stranger dressed in black was named Lassiter and could draw a gun faster than any other man alive. They all agreed that the gamblers had provoked the fight, and though Lassiter had tried to talk them out of going for their guns, they had all been intent on killing him.

Lund knew that this gunfighter named Lassiter had certainly shot in self-defense. But the sheriff had wanted to take Lassiter in anyway, to show that he could handle anyone who came along. That hadn't happened with the black-clothed gunfighter.

As Lund now kicked his horse into a run toward Porter Draw, he could once again see Lassiter looking over at him through the haze of blue smoke, and then stepping over the bodies, out of the saloon. No one had blamed him for not trying to stop Lassiter and take him in, but it had left a sore spot within Lund. To his way of thinking, it had made him appear small in the eyes of the townspeople. He hadn't even tried to take the gunfighter in. Maybe Lassiter would have gotten off; but he hadn't even gone to jail.

Now Lund found himself hoping this was the same man. And he hoped that Hardy Malone had not yet hanged him. Lund wanted a chance to get him into his jail here in Cheyenne—to make up for that time back in Abilene.

Hardy Malone was standing in front of Lassiter with the other two cowhands, telling him again that he was going to be hanged. Malone and the other two had spent some time looking over Lassiter's black stallion. They had even cut cards to see who would claim him. Malone had won.

Now Malone was ready to finish the job. He told one of the other two hands to get a rope.

Lassiter continued to stand wth his hands raised, insisting to the three that they would be making a mistake by attempting to hang him. Finally, he saw there was no deterring these men from their ambition, and decided he no longer had time to talk to them.

Malone moved two steps forward and lowered his rifle, so that he could look into Lassiter's eyes.

"You prefer any particular tree in this draw?" he said mockingly. "Pick one which suits your fancy."

Determined not to be hanged by these men, nor anyone else, Lassiter decided if his time had come, he would go out fighting.

With a powerful stroke, Lassiter brought down his hands and smashed a fist directly into Hardy Malone's mouth. Malone's head snapped back and he sprawled backward to the ground, dropping his rifle.

The other two were taken by surprise, and before they could react, Lassiter leaped and picked up his two revolvers. He had them cocked, pointed at the two men.

"Drop those rifles or use them," Lassiter challenged. "And throw that rope over here to me."

The two cowhands, staring in bewilderment, looked at each other and to their rifles, then dropped them. The one with the rope threw it at Lassiter's feet.

Malone was getting up from the ground, yelling at them.

"What'd you two do that for? He can't get all three of us."

"Maybe not, but you'll be first to go," Lassiter promised him.

Malone was holding his mouth, his lips split. They were beginning to swell, blood trailing down across his chin. The way he was testing the inside of his mouth,

Lassiter knew he had loosened a few of Malone's teeth as well.

"Maybe I should put this rope around *your* neck," Lassiter suggested to Malone.

Malone backed up a few steps to where the other two hands were still staring at Lassiter.

"You'd better let us go," Malone said.

Lassiter shook his head. "Not a chance."

"What do you plan to do with us?" one of the other two asked Lassiter.

"Just let me think on it," Lassiter said. "You were all going to hang me. I don't think I should let you off very easy, do you?"

A strained expression of fear crept over the faces of the two cowhands. Malone's face just showed anger.

"You're in deep and you're gettin' in deeper," Malone told Lassiter. "We'll have a posse after you in no time."

"You're the one who should be worried," Lassiter replied. "You don't want anyone to know that it was you who killed this man, do you?" Lassiter was pointing to the body on the ground near them, looking hard at Malone and sensing his sudden fear.

"What are you talkin' about?" Malone demanded.

"I think you know," Lassiter said. "You shot him while I was talking to him. You didn't expect me to be here. So you had to try and get me as well. When you didn't get the job done, you figured the next best thing would be to try and frame me."

The other two hands were looking at Malone now, wondering if what this gunfighter dressed in black was saying had any truth to it.

"He's a liar! Can't you see that?" Malone was spitting as he fumed, blood still running from his lips.

The sounds of more horsemen could be heard coming toward the crossing. Malone turned and thought about going for his gun. Lassiter cocked both pistols and pointed one directly at Hardy's midsection, then told the other two not to move.

Lassiter kept the three covered and waited until the riders reined in their horses. It was two cowhands and three other men. One of them was wearing a badge.

"What's going on here?" Frank Lund demanded.

Lassiter had seen a lot of faces in a lot of towns, some for just a short time. He didn't know when or in what town, but he knew he had seen this marshal before.

"This man is a killer," Malone spoke up quickly, pointing at Lassiter. "He shot Allen Hutton and now he figures to do us in. Good thing you got here."

"The way I heard it, you were about to hang him," Lund commented. He turned to Johnny and the other cowhand. "Isn't that what you told me?"

Johnny Ridge nodded. "That's right."

Malone glared at Johnny Ridge. "You yellow-bellied scum!" he slurred.

"Just cool off Malone," Lund ordered. "I've got things in hand here now."

"He deserves to be strung up," Malone said to the lawman, pointing at Lassiter.

"I told you I've got charge of things here," Lund told Malone again. Lund then turned to Lassiter. "The best thing you can do now is just hand those two pistols of yours up to me and come along peacefully."

Lassiter had expected to be taken into custody. But he didn't want to take the chance of being unarmed around Malone.

"Just so you take everyone's guns at the same time," Lassiter told Lund.

The marshal studied Malone and the other two a

moment. Finally, he ordered the three men to get on their horses and ride back to the ranch where they worked. He told Johnny Ridge and the other hand to go with them.

"I'll take care of this stranger," Lund finished.

"You'll need all of us to make certain he doesn't get away," Malone protested. "And what about Allen Hutton's body?"

"You heard what I said, Malone," Lund said gruffly. "Do as you're told. I don't need you to help me. I've got deputies."

Malone grumbled some more as he and the other two climbed onto their horses and left. Johnny Ridge and the other hand told Lund they weren't going back to the ranch with Malone. They would go into town and leave at their own discretion.

"Malone's certain to have it in for me now," Johnny Ridge said.

"Suit yourself," Lund told him. He talked as he got down from his horse and took Lassiter's rifle and pistols from him. "Just head on out."

Lassiter watched Johnny Ridge and the other hand head for town, while the two deputies and Lund stayed behind. Lund then tied Lassiter's hands behind him with a length of rope and helped Lassiter onto his black stallion.

"You don't need to go through all this," Lassiter protested. "You've got my guns."

"I'm not taking any chances," Lund said. He looked to the two deputies. "I'll go ahead with this stranger. You two get Hutton's body back on his horse and catch up with us."

"Don't you want help with him?" one of the deputies asked, pointing at Lassiter.

"He's not going anywhere," Lund said.

The two deputies got busy loading Allen Hutton's body onto the bay stallion. Lassiter sat in the saddle, his hands tied securely, while Lund led his black stallion toward town.

"What are you doing in the territory?" Lund asked Lassiter.

"I came to ride for Jack Stanford in the Fourth of July horse race," Lassiter replied.

"I see," Lund said, nodding. "Stanford's having a hard time. He's a squatter. The bigger stockmen don't like him. He should move on. You tell him that."

Lund could see that Lassiter was visibly angered at what he had just said and at having to go into town when Hardy Malone and the other two were freed without even so much as questioning.

"What's the favoritism for?" Lassiter asked Lund. "Those three—especially Malone—had just as big a part in all this as me."

"Malone was with the others, and they work for the Box Y," Lund told Lassiter. "Trace McCord has a big herd of cattle and a powerful influence around here. I can't hold his men unless I'm *certain* they committed some crime."

"What makes you so certain *I* committed this murder?" Lassiter asked the marshal.

"I'm certain you *didn't* commit this murder," Lund said flatly. "You're a professional. You would be ten miles from here by now had you shot Hutton. But you're the stranger around here, and I have to take you in. Besides, I think it makes us even for a time some years back."

"Some years back?" Lassiter was confused.

"Yeah, when you shot three men and then just walked past me," Lund said. "Think for a while.

You'll remember in time. You made me look bad, Lassiter."

Lassiter thought hard, but couldn't remember the incident Lund was talking about. Whatever had happened, Lund had apparently taken it personally.

"You should have let me take you in back then," Lund said. "I might have just let you go right away, but you should have let me take you in. This time I'm taking you in, and I doubt if you'll get out of my jail alive."

4

LASSITER LOOKED OUT FROM behind the bars and into the street. The crowd was still gathered, talking about him and the shooting death of Allen Hutton. It sounded now like they all wanted to hang him just as bad as Hardy Malone had earlier. And the reason was plain—Hardy Malone was in the middle of them, doing most of the talking.

Malone had ridden right into town from Porter Draw and had gotten the townspeople angered immediately. If it hadn't been for Frank Lund's yelling at them upon first entering town, they would have dragged Lassiter from his horse.

Lund had made it clear immediately that anyone interfering with the law and the way he administered it was going to join Lassiter in jail. He had even threatened Malone with a stint behind bars if he didn't back off and leave well enough alone.

It was plain to Lassiter that he had gotten himself in the middle of a power play between Frank Lund and

Hardy Malone. Neither man was willing to give in to the other if he didn't have to. The only reason Malone was backing down, Lassiter knew, was because Lund was wearing a badge.

The friction between the two of them was no doubt going to become stronger. Lassiter concluded that he might eventually be able to use that friction to work the two men against one another and, hopefully, get himself out of the mess he was now in. If he could get Lund to believe that Malone had killed Allen Hutton, things could change.

From the looks of things, Allen Hutton had been one of the most popular cowhands in the area, liked by everyone. On the way back to town, Lund had mentioned more than once that Allen Hutton's murder was going to be a lot more complicated than just an ordinary shooting. It was going to be like setting off a charge of gunpowder in the middle of town.

Lund had already explained to Lassiter that Trace McCord and his Box Y outfit was the biggest in the valley. Allen Hutton had been McCord's best hand, and was going to race the blood bay for McCord in the big Fourth of July event. But these facts were only a minor part of the complications that would come with his death. More important, Hutton had been engaged to marry McCord's daughter Clara on the day of the race.

"Try explaining to McCord and his daughter that you didn't kill Allen Hutton," Lund had told Lassiter just before reaching town. "I sure wouldn't want to be you."

Clara McCord was Trace McCord's only child, born in Virginia to him and his wife, Mary Ellen, who had died of cholera when Clara was sixteen. The Civil War had just ended, and McCord's fortune had been stolen by carpetbaggers. After the death of his wife, he decided to leave the past behind and start fresh in the open plains of the West.

Determined not to have his possessions stolen ever again, McCord had turned hard and mean. He built his empire rapidly and fought to expand. Those in his way were crushed, and no one saw any reason why he shouldn't run his outfit any way he wanted to.

Clara was now *the* woman of Cheyenne. Everyone knew her and noted her presence—especially the trail-weary cowhands who came and went regularly. But Trace McCord kept a tight rein on his daughter—as tight as he possibly could—and most often nobody got near enough to say hello.

Allen Hutton had come along and changed all that. Their romance had bloomed rapidly, as Hutton was a flashy rider and maintained a dignity that interested Trace McCord. Hutton had come from expensive Eastern blood and had told McCord more than once that his family could help the Box Y expand clear into Montana and Idaho territories.

A fearless and flashy young rider was what Trace McCord had always wanted for Clara. Allen Hutton was that man. But now he was dead.

As he continued to look out through the cell window, Lassiter couldn't help thinking that the cards were stacked heavily against him. And Frank Lund was playing it safe, because he wanted to get even for something he didn't like that had happened a number of years ago in Abilene.

Lund was now sitting at his desk, catching up on what he had missed in the newspapers. Though edgy about what was happening with Malone and the others in the street, he tried to appear calm. Lund wasn't unhappy about the prospect that Lassiter would likely hang; he just didn't want to have to face Hardy Malone if there was going to be gunplay.

Lassiter new Lund wished Trace McCord would hurry up and get into town. He should have arrived by now. When he came, it would take the pressure off Lund and allow him to run things the way McCord wanted. And he knew McCord wouldn't want Hardy Malone doing the hanging on his own.

It bothered Lassiter to think that he might be led to a gallows just for convenience sake, that Lund was just stepping out of the way while the town turned against the wrong man.

Lassiter turned from the cell window and stared at Lund reading his paper. The marshal didn't want to talk to Lassiter any more than he absolutely had to. He wouldn't discuss Hardy Malone or Allen Hutton at any length, only to confirm that Trace McCord and his daughter would want to know who killed Allen Hutton and why. Then they would want to see that man hang.

Lassiter was now convinced that his only way out of this was to escape. But that wouldn't be easy. And from the looks of things in the street, he might not have enough time to even consider a plan to get out.

He watched Hardy Malone point and continue to incite the crowd against him. The anger was growing by the minute, and Lassiter could see that Lund was thinking about getting up from his chair and quieting them.

Then things changed suddenly. Lassiter turned back to the street and saw Malone and the others turn and move out of the way as two riders came hurriedly into town.

It was a middle-aged man and a striking woman in her early twenties. Lassiter knew he was watching Trace McCord and his daughter as they slowed their horses to a trot and headed for the jail.

There was a lot of talk and pointing from the crowd as Hardy Malone and the others watched from the side of the street. Trace McCord was in the lead, a tall and rawboned cattleman in middle age, whose face now showed intense anger through the lines that had come from years of riding in the wind. He didn't even bother to look at Hardy Malone and the others, but stared ahead at the jail.

Clara McCord was astonishingly beautiful. Long, light blond hair was braided and tied in a bun behind her head and pinned under a dark blue, lace-edged hat. She wore a navy-blue, split riding skirt, and blue gloves to match. Up close or far away, the woman was stunning. And Lassiter could see, even from that distance, that her face was tearstained.

Lassiter turned from the window and watched Lund get up from his desk and prepare himself to meet the McCords. He straightened his shoulders and adjusted his gun belt. He placed his hat on his head two or three times, until it felt right, then took a quick look at Lassiter before going out.

McCord spoke as soon as he saw Lund appear. His voice was gruff and loud, even from outside the jail.

"I want to see him," he said as he dismounted.

A few moments later Lassiter was staring into the hateful eyes of the big cattleman. Clara was standing behind her father, drying her eyes. She didn't want to even look at the prisoner.

McCord continued to glare at Lassiter, while Frank Lund took a position near the doorway. Lassiter met McCord's gaze with absolutely no fear; and after the two men had sized each other up, it was McCord who spoke first.

"Why did you kill him?"

"It wasn't me," Lassiter answered. "I'm tired of saying it to everybody."

"So why are you behind bars?"

"It looks to me like I'm the convenient one to pin it

on," Lassiter replied. He looked over at Lund and added, "The law in this town wants to make me pay for something that happened in the past—something he says I did that made him unhappy."

McCord turned to Lund. Lassiter saw Clara looking at Lund as well, wondering what Lassiter was talking about.

"What's he talking about?" McCord asked. "Did you two have a run-in some years back?"

Lund nodded. "Back in Abilene. I was a deputy. He killed three gamblers and hurried out of town. He was an outlaw then. He's an outlaw now."

Suddenly it all came back to Lassiter. The barroom, the three gamblers intent on killing him to cover up a secret. Lassiter smiled to himself. He remembered the secret. It might be worth bringing up to Frank Lund later.

"I don't know what that has to do with this," McCord said, turning back to Lassiter.

Lassiter smiled with confidence. "I'm just trying to show that your marshal isn't following the intent of the law, which makes a man innocent until proven guilty."

"Every guilty man says he's innocent," McCord said.

"And a lot of innocent men have the same attitude," Lassiter pointed out.

"So, why does everyone think you killed Allen, then?" McCord asked. "Why is everyone so sure about it?"

Lassiter pointed out into the street. "Everyone saw Lund bring me in—with my hands tied—as if he had caught me in the act. Isn't that reason enough?"

"Frank brought you in because he thinks you're guilty," McCord stated. He turned to Lund. "That right, Frank?"

"He's the number-one suspect," Lund answered.

"Well, I'm not the number-one suspect," Lassiter said quickly. "I can say without question that a man named Hardy Malone was the one who shot him."

"Hardy Malone?" McCord was squinting. "What makes you so sure?"

"Because Allen Hutton was shot in the back while he was talking to me," Lassiter told him. "Then whoever shot him tried to get me. When I went after him, he hightailed it. Then, suddenly, Malone appears all sweated up and tells the cowhands with him he saw me shoot Allen Hutton."

"Why would Malone want to kill him?" McCord asked.

"I don't know," Lassiter explained. "Whatever reason, Malone was hired by somebody to kill this man to keep him out of the upcoming race. Malone didn't realize someone else would be in Porter Draw, but he shot anyway. I chased him off, and he came back with some of his friends. They were going to lynch me, but Lund showed up with his deputies."

"Sounds like a made-up story to me," McCord said.

"I've told you what happened," Lassiter said flatly. "So decide what you want."

McCord turned back to Lund again. "What about this story?"

"That's what he told me," Lund said with a shrug. "He was holding his guns on Hardy Malone and two of your hands when I got to him with my deputies. Malone said he saw him kill Allen. He's the only witness."

"That makes it real comfortable for Malone," Lassiter said. "He's well-known around here. I'm not."

McCord turned back to Lassiter and squinted. "I still don't know why Malone would want to kill Allen.

Malone has shown interest in going to work for me. Why would he want to kill one of my hands?"

"I can't answer that," Lassiter replied. "But he sure brought your hands down to that crossing quick. And he sure wants me to hang real fast, so there won't be any more questions."

McCord still had his hands on his hips. He studied Lassiter closely.

"What are you doing around here?"

"I intend to ride in the Fourth of July race for Jack Stanford."

Lassiter could hear Clara McCord, standing behind her father, crying in her handkerchief again. She would have turned away and walked outside, but there was a crowd gathering in front of the jail.

McCord turned to his daughter for a moment, then looked back to Lassiter.

"I might have considered believing you if you hadn't told me you came to ride for Jack Stanford," he finally said. "Stanford's a thief. So I don't think that makes you much better than him. And to look at you, I'd say he might have hired you to kill Allen. I'll see to it that you hang."

McCord then turned and escorted his daughter out of the jail. Clara stopped once and looked back at Lassiter before leaving with her father. Lund didn't bother to look at Lassiter at all as he followed the two out into the street.

Lund made the crowd move aside as McCord and his daughter mounted their horses. Even from where Lassiter stood at his jail-cell door, he could hear McCord's gruff voice echoing through the streets, addressing Hardy Malone and the crowd.

"That stranger inside there will pay for his crime. He will have a fair trial, then he will hang. Don't anybody mess this up by trying to lynch him ahead of time. He'll go to the gallows when the time is right."

Lassiter heard the crowd yelling their approval. As Lassiter moved to the window, he could see McCord and his daughter riding out of town. At the edge of the street Hardy Malone watched them, then led a group of cowhands into a saloon.

Lund came back into the jail and sat down at his desk. Lassiter recalled the incident in Abilene once again and wondered why Lund had even brought it up. Lund certainly wouldn't have said a word if he had any idea what Lassiter knew about the connection between Frank Lund and those three gamblers.

Lassiter waited until Lund had gotten settled with the paper again.

"Want to come in here a minute, Lund?" Lassiter called to him.

Lund didn't even look up from his paper. "I have nothing to discuss with you."

"Maybe there are some things about your time in Abilene that McCord would be interested in knowing," Lassiter said.

Lund looked up. "What are you talking about?"

"I'm talking about the payoffs you got from the Stevens gang when they robbed the bank that summer afternoon," Lassiter said.

Lund appeared stunned. He put his paper down and came in to where Lassiter stood calmly looking out the window.

"What are you talking about?" Lund asked.

"Why do you think those gamblers tried to kill me?" Lassiter asked. "They knew I'd heard from one of the gang members about you, a man I fought in the war with. They had already killed him. They were trying to get me, or didn't you know that?"

Lund had a look of surprise, and then fear, on his face.

"If you think for a minute I'll walk to a gallows peacefully, you've got another think coming," Lassiter advised him. "You better look into Hardy Malone a lot more closely than you have."

Lassiter saw the marshal blink quickly, the sharp fear penetrating deep into him. Lund knew he couldn't just kill Lassiter; that would make McCord wonder, and it would make him extremely mad. McCord wanted to see Lassiter hang, and he wanted to do it himself.

Lund knew now that he had to come up with something to either delay the trial or the hanging. He was caught between McCord and Lassiter, and he was certain that one man could make things just as difficult as the other.

5

THE COMMOTION IN THE STREET over Lassiter had died down, but Hardy Malone wasn't content to let things rest. Whether or not Trace McCord wanted Lassiter for himself, Malone didn't want to wait to see Lassiter hang.

He sat in the saloon with five of the Box Y cowhands, telling them that the stranger dressed in black was as dangerous a man as had ever come into the valley. Malone poured whiskey for the hands while they listened. He wasn't willing to reconsider letting Lassiter have even the rest of the day before he died.

"I say we're taking a big chance by letting that murderer breathe at all," Malone was saying. "If he don't hang right away, sure as hell he'll get out and kill somebody else."

Malone poured another round while the Box Y hands spoke among themselves. Malone didn't work for the outfit, and they were all wondering why he was advocating a lynching only minutes after Trace

McCord had spoken about leaving Lassiter alone until the time was right.

Malone set the bottle down and looked at the hands. "I say we get him out and string him up, like we planned before Frank Lund spoiled it."

"There ain't no way we're going to see him hang until McCord's ready," one of the hands pointed out. "No use to keep stirring people up."

"You don't understand," Malone said. "That gunfighter's got nothing to lose. He's liable to lie his way out of it. Then what?"

"He ain't going to lie his way past Trace McCord," another hand put in.

The other hands, nodding, agreed. They were content knowing that Lassiter would hang when their boss wanted it to happen.

Malone took a deep breath and poured down a whiskey. He thought a moment. There had to be a way to stir them into some kind of action, he thought. Finally he brought up Jack Stanford.

"Word is, that gunfighter came to town to work for Jack Stanford," Malone said. "Maybe we'd ought to ask Stanford some questions."

"He's nothing to worry about," one of the hands said. "He's just a squatter. He's having a tough time making it. He'll be gone before the summer's over."

"What I'm trying to say," Malone told the hand, leaning over the table, "is that this gunfighter likely came here to help Stanford get on his feet—you know, steal horses or something like that."

"If Stanford was a thief, McCord would have had him hanged," the hand said. "But he didn't, so we ain't sure about it."

Malone drank, and wiped whiskey from his chin with his forearm. "You ain't listening to me. I'm saying Stanford has to do something to make it here. He's thinking that horse race will bring in a lot of money to the winner. It's for certain Stanford put that stranger up to killing Allen Hutton, so that stranger could win the race.''

The hands shook their heads, still not convinced that Malone had a good argument. They were getting ready to leave when the batwing doors swung open and Johnny Ridge came in with the other cowhand who had ridden to tell Frank Lund about the lynching plan. From the look on Johnny's face, he appeared to have something to say. The cowhands sat tight.

Johnny was well aware that Malone was staring hard at him. But he wasn't going to let that keep him from telling the other Box Y hands what he had heard. He walked up to the table with the other hand and looked down at Malone.

"You've got a lot of nerve comin' in here like this," Malone told Johnny. "After you stuck up for that killer, stranger and all."

"Who's to say he's the killer?" Johnny retorted. "You? You're the only one who saw it. Who's to say you're not the one lying about the whole thing?"

Malone's face turned deep red. "What are you trying to say?" Malone asked.

"Everyone wants to know why Allen Hutton was killed," Johnny said. "A lot of people think it was because he was likely to win the horse race on that blood bay of his. But it seems funny that somebody didn't kill him way before now, if that was the case. I heard something else."

Malone leaned forward in his chair, trying to hide the concern that crept into his face.

"There's word going around that Allen Hutton had talked about somebody being after him for a long time.

Something about a Yankee from the war looking for him, for killing his brother when some battle was over."

Everyone was silent, looking hard at Johnny. After another moment of silence, Johnny looked at Malone.

"Did you have a brother killed by Allen Hutton in the war?"

"No," Malone said flatly.

Johnny looked to the hand standing right beside him. "Curly, didn't you tell me awhile ago that Malone told you he had a younger brother that got killed by a coward bluebelly Yankee at Shiloh?"

The hand nodded.

Malone rose from his chair, his hand hovering above his gun. He was looking at both Johnny and the other cowhand.

"You two calling me a liar?" he blurted.

Johnny stood firm. "Go ahead and shoot us if you want. But it will be in cold blood, and you'll be in jail with that gunfighter. I don't think you want that."

Malone stood staring at Johnny, then blinked a few times. He hadn't thought of going to jail with Lassiter. That wouldn't be a good idea.

But Malone had to save face now. He noticed all the Box Y hands staring at him, and scattered throughout the bar, hands from various other outfits as well. He had let his temper get the best of him.

"A man don't like to be thought of as a liar, Johnny," Malone said, sitting back down. "You can understand that. I didn't mean to get riled. Have a seat and drink a whiskey with us."

Johnny ignored the offer. "Maybe we had all better look pretty hard at Mr. Malone, here, before we go to pointing any fingers," Johnny continued.

Then he and the other hand turned and walked out

of the saloon. Everyone watched. Then a few of the other Box Y hands who had been sitting at the table with Malone got up and left too. Everyone in the saloon was talking.

Finally, Malone tried to get things back to normal by proposing a toast on behalf of the Box Y and many good years in the cattle business. Those left at the table drank, but not with the enthusiasm they would have had before Johnny Ridge and the other hand came in. Things had changed.

Before long the rest of the Box Y hands left the table. Most were headed back to the ranch, while others went to different saloons. The talk was going with them. Malone knew Johnny Ridge had really stirred things up.

Malone drank by himself and wondered if he couldn't have planned things a little better. But how was he to know the stranger dressed in black would show up? At first it looked as if it would be a perfect setup—having the stranger there so it looked like he had pulled the trigger. Now, however, it seemed to Malone that he should have put the shooting off until another time. He should have waited until the stranger was at least settled in the valley at Jack Stanford's place. That would have made it look better.

He had wanted to kill Hutton for a lot of years, and had finally caught up with him. If only he could have waited just a few more days, or if the stranger hadn't been there. But it was over now, and things were getting hard.

Malone shook his head as he drank. It had been perfect, with the horse race and all. Hutton had been a shoo-in as the winner. There were likely a lot of people who didn't want Hutton to ride. It would have

looked like a lot of people had a motive to do him in—
especially for that kind of money.

Now Johnny Ridge and this other hand named Curly
were making him look bad. And it was certain they
would continue to talk. Malone couldn't have that. He
would have to do something about it, and soon. He
couldn't afford to have anyone wondering about him
now, not even a little bit.

Clara McCord dried her eyes and stared out into the
corral. The blood bay was circling nervously, snorting
and throwing its head around. Since getting back from
town, Clara had been at the corral without taking her
eyes off the horse. That had been nearly two hours
before, and it was getting close to dark. But Clara
didn't care; she had no place she wanted to be.

She knew that even the bay stallion would never be
the same. Things had changed forever. The stallion
seemed nervous, anxious, and almost uncontrollable,
now that its accustomed rider was no longer around.

Allen Hutton had taken the stallion as a colt, had
broken and trained it. The only other person the
stallion would tolerate on its back was Clara. She had
ridden double with Allen numerous times. And just
two days before, she had ridden him by herself.

She and Allen had laughed together and hugged one
another. The stallion had finally accepted her, as he
had Allen. But now she didn't want to ride the horse,
not ever again.

Her future seemed an open blank. She had no idea
what she wanted to do with her life. She loved her
father dearly, and the ranch as well. She loved the
land and the legacy of the valley, but she had loved
Allen Hutton more than anything she could ever imag-

ine, and now he was gone. She didn't know if she could stand to face the empty memories.

She thought of the options. She could leave and go back East. But who did she know there now? Neither her father nor her deceased mother had had any brothers or sisters. Her grandparents on both sides were dead as well. She might have distant relatives, but would they care about her?

And what could she do? All she had ever known since coming to the mountains was the wide-open spaces of the Box Y. She didn't feel she could ever get that out of her blood.

Besides, going to a place where nobody knew her would be an entirely empty life. And she loved her father deeply and didn't want to leave him.

She continued to wonder about the future, watching the stallion pacing, pacing, pacing. Allen's burial was set for tomorrow. The sun was now setting. Clara had almost hoped she wouldn't wake up to see it rise again.

Her mind wandered back to the jail, where the stranger dressed in black was no doubt looking out the cell window into the street, watching the sunset. Though he had been able to hold it well, she had been able to see the intense frustration in his eyes. He had been like a caged cat.

That, in itself, had made her wonder. Why would a man take the chance of killing someone in cold blood out in the open? And what would make him want to kill Allen? He was no doubt a gunfighter, and had killed often enough before, but to shoot a man off his horse for no apparent motive seemed very odd. A man like that would think too much of his freedom to take drastic chances with it.

As she mused, she heard her father come up behind her. He was quiet as he leaned his big forearms against the corral poles next to her and watched the stallion's nervous pacing. Finally he spoke.

"I'm sorry about what happened, Clara. But there's nothing either of us can do. We've got to go on. We can hang that stranger and then forget about it."

"I don't think he killed Allen," she said calmly.

Trace McCord turned quickly to his daughter. "What do you mean?"

"I mean, I think someone else killed Allen. Someone else who had a good reason."

"Malone said he thought the stranger killed Allen so he wouldn't win the big race. That sounds reasonable to me."

"I don't think that stranger would ride into this or any other valley just to kill someone he didn't know," Clara said.

"Do you believe all of what that stranger said about Hardy Malone?" McCord asked his daughter. "Is that what you're saying?"

"I don't know what to believe about Hardy Malone," she said. "After all, what *do* we know about him? He's just as much a stranger as that Lassiter is."

McCord thought a moment. He realized that his daughter had a point, that Hardy Malone's past was a mystery to everybody. Malone had taken it upon himself in the short time he had been in the valley to become popular among the cowhands and the townsfolk alike. But no one really knew who he was.

"Maybe it was Malone, maybe it was somebody else," Clara went on. "But I think that stranger is innocent."

"Why do you think so?"

"Because of the way he looked at me. He acted like he knew just how I felt, like he had had the same experience at one time in his life."

"Maybe he was hired to kill Allen and had no idea that Allen was engaged to you."

"I don't think he's the kind of man who would shoot somebody in the back. The way he talked to you, he had nothing to be ashamed of and didn't care whether we believed him or not."

Trace McCord was silent for a time longer. He watched the stallion again, thinking. He wondered why his daughter would be so certain about a stranger she had never met before, someone who certainly had killed and was dressed to kill again. It didn't make sense to him.

But then again, he knew that his daughter always had hunches about things and that she was usually right. Maybe it was that way with this stranger too. Maybe. But again, maybe not.

6

LASSITER STOOD AT THE CELL WINDOW, watching the sun fall across the mountains a good distance to the west. Dried grass and sage covered the hills that spread far toward the mountains, the brittle stalks bathed now in a gold sheen that made the land appear as if it were glowing.

The heat of the day still lingered in Lassiter's cell. Though the sun would soon be setting and a crimson light would fall on the town, Lassiter was in no mood to enjoy the beauty. He wasn't out of jail yet. And he certainly wasn't used to spending his evenings behind bars, especially after being framed for a murder.

The events of the day had developed so quickly that it was hard for him to put it all together. The combination of Hardy Malone and Frank Lund, both of whom were so desperate to hide their pasts, was going to make it hard for him to stay out of a noose. But with some deep thinking and a little luck, Lassiter knew he would find an opening.

He would have to find a way to show Malone as the killer, he thought. He was going to have to turn it around so that people knew Malone had framed him. It was hard enough to understand how Hardy Malone could have gotten back to Porter Draw fast enough to make it appear as if he had committed the crime, but it was even harder to figure how Malone had convinced so many people that he was helping the whole valley by getting rid of a stranger nobody knew.

After thinking on it, Lassiter realized that the young cowboy, Johnny Ridge, had to have some deep suspicions regarding Malone. Ridge had taken it upon himself, with another hand, to ride to town and get the law. Something had made him think that Malone was trying too hard for a lynching. Lassiter was glad for the cowhand's concern but he wasn't exactly fond of the lawman Ridge had brought to establish law and order.

Finding out about Lund's underhanded operation in Abilene those years back had been more a matter of luck than detective work. One of the gamblers Lassiter had later shot had blurted during a card game that he wasn't about to worry about losing a few hundred dollars that night—that plenty was coming in later. Lassiter followed the gambler to a meeting with Frank Lund and the others. The saloon had been crowded and noisy, and Lassiter hadn't heard what was said, but had realized what was going on when the bank fell the next morning.

The robbery had occurred bright and early. Lund was conveniently out of town, even though the main marshal was off serving a warrant. Later in the day Lassiter confronted the gambler who had been trying to cheat him during a card game, and confirmed for himself Lund's involvement. Afterward the other gamblers killed their fellow gang members, which led to Lassiter's shootout in the saloon.

Now, Lassiter couldn't figure why Lund was making such a fuss over not having taken him to jail for it. Certainly Lund wouldn't have wanted the news of his association with the robbery getting out. But then, Lund seemed more concerned with his image as a lawman than as a gentleman, an aspect of him that hadn't changed at all.

Lassiter, who could now hear Lund coming from the other room again, turned from the window. Lund was carrying a lantern against the shadows that had crept into the jail's interior. He stopped at the cell door and stared in at Lassiter for a moment.

"I've been thinking about what you knew about me while I was a deputy in Abilene," he told Lassiter, the light flickering off his face. "And I've decided that you can go right ahead and tell McCord about it if you want. I don't care."

Lassiter stood silent. Lund waited for him to speak or react in some way. Finally, he continued.

"You see, it's your word against mine. And a man about to hang will come up with almost anything to save his own hide."

Lassiter remained silent. He turned and looked out the window again, where the sun continued to fall behind the western horizon.

Lund became exasperated. "Why don't you say something?"

Lassiter turned. "What do you want me to say? Maybe I'll tell them anyway. It won't hurt to try."

"Try all you want," Lund said. "McCord is on my side. Especially after you told him you intended to ride in the Fourth of July race for Jack Stanford."

Lassiter remembered Trace McCord's angry reaction at hearing Jack Stanford's name earlier. McCord had even gone so far as to call Stanford a thief. Lassiter wondered about that. Maybe Lund could shed some light on what had made McCord react that way.

"What's wrong with Jack Stanford?" Lassiter asked. "I heard McCord say he was not liked in this town."

Lund grunted. "Jack Stanford doesn't have a lot, but he's scratching. McCord and the other big ranchers see him as a threat. They've been able to pretty much run off the other smaller ranchers, but Stanford is kind of a hitch in their side—a burr under their saddle, so to speak."

"This is all government land," Lassiter pointed out. "No one has a right to lay claim to any grazing rights."

"You know what happens, Lassiter," Lund said, annoyed. "The biggest and the strongest survive. The others get pushed out."

"But Jack Stanford isn't like the other smaller ranchers," Lassiter said. "Is that it? He doesn't bow down to McCord?"

"Something like that," McCord said.

Lassiter nodded. He understood. That was the Jack Stanford he knew; somebody who couldn't be pushed around. It sounded as if Trace McCord was having a real hard time getting rid of Stanford, and now thought Lassiter was here to help with things.

"So now McCord thinks Stanford hired me to help him, is that it?" Lassiter asked.

"You're a smart man, Lassiter," Lund stated with a smile. "Too bad you'll have to die. You should have found out about Stanford before you came all the way up here."

Lassiter decided that Lund was now also thinking that Stanford had hired him to come into the valley and fight the big ranchers with him. Either that or Lund didn't care one way or another and was just glad McCord had another reason to see him hang.

"You see how it is?" Lund said again. "You'd just as well decide that your last days have arrived."

"You're taking a lot for granted, Lund," Lassiter said flatly. "I'm a long ways from the gallows."

"Not really," Lund said quickly. "And I would bet good money we'll just get Jack Stanford at the same time. Maybe we'll even string him up on the same day. A double treat for the folks." He laughed.

"Just because Jack Stanford doesn't do what McCord wants him to is no reason to call him a thief," Lassiter pointed out.

"It's more than that," Lund said. "There's talk he's taken to stealing horses. That's a mistake around here."

"Talk is all it is, I'd bet," Lassiter said. "Anybody who's trying to stand up for himself against the rest will sooner or later have some charge trumped up against him."

Lund laughed again. "It doesn't matter to me what you say, or to Trace McCord, either, for that matter. Like I said, Stanford and you will look at the end of a rope together."

"And I've told you, I haven't been hanged yet," Lassiter said with conviction. "And I don't intend to be."

"How do you expect to avoid it?" Lund asked.

"Maybe it will come as a surprise to you," Lassiter said.

Lund was confident that Lassiter couldn't make anyone believe anything about his days as a deputy in Abilene. Not now, especially since Lassiter had admitted being tied in with Jack Stanford. Nevertheless,

Lund was uneasy. He knew as long as Lassiter was alive, anything could happen.

"There's too much in your past for you to hide it all," Lassiter told Lund, taking advantage of Lund's apparent unease.

Lund moved from one foot to another, staring at Lassiter through the shadows. "I hope you do tell McCord about Abilene," he finally said. "I want to see it when he laughs in your face."

Lund turned and went back to his desk without another word, leaving Lassiter in the waning light of late evening. Lassiter didn't call him back; he knew Lund had a point. No one was likely to take his word over Lund's, especially McCord.

Lund rummaged about his desk and did nervous work until he finally decided to leave the jail. He took his hat from a nail on the wall and blew out the lantern. He was trying to make himself feel better about the situation with Lassiter, working to convince himself that Trace McCord could care less about anything that Lassiter had to tell him. But it was hard to be sure about it.

Lund decided he was going over to have a drink and try to relax. A circuit judge would be in town in less than a week. Then everything would be over until the day of the hanging.

As he turned for the door, Lund took a deep breath. He was aware that Lassiter was staring at him in the near darkness. But he made himself ignore it and told himself things were under control. Lassiter would never leave his jail, except to go to the gallows.

He had also relaxed his concern about Hardy Malone leading a lynch mob; there weren't many in this town who wanted to go against Trace McCord's wishes. Lassiter would hang and McCord would have a front-row seat.

But a visitor met him at the door to the jail, just as darkness was almost complete. Lund stepped back inside and removed his hat. He stammered with surprise as he spoke.

"Miss McCord. I certainly didn't expect you. Where's your father?"

"I don't always travel with my father," Clara said. "I've come to see the accused man. Mr. Lassiter, I believe is his name."

"Are you sure your father would approve?" Lund asked.

Clara McCord looked directly into Lund's eyes. Even in the dim light, Lund could see them flashing.

"I'll tell you what, Mr. Lund," she said flatly, "why don't you just ride out to the ranch and ask him. If you don't think I'm old enough to be about my own affairs, then you had better think again."

Lund apologized and backed farther into the office. Clara stared at him while he took the glass chimney off the lantern on his desk and struck light to it once again.

"Are you sure you want to go back there?" Lund asked Clara. "That man is dangerous."

Clara narrowed her eyes once again. "I don't have all evening, Mr. Lund."

Lund resented the fact that Clara always referred to him as Mister instead of Marshal Lund. Lund took it to mean she didn't respect him enough to think of him as a man of the law.

He was right. Clara didn't think much of him at all. She had been suspicious of Lund the first time she had seen her father talking with him. She knew how her father controlled things in the valley, and she could see immediately that Lund would do anything he was told.

Though she admired her father and respected his judgment—for the most part—she realized that Lund would never take it upon himself to stand up for what he knew was right, even if it meant saving a man's life.

Lund cleared his throat and escorted Clara back to where Lassiter stood at the window of his cell.

Clara watched the shadows of the lantern dance off his tall, strong frame. He seemed as detached from everything as he had the first time she had seen him.

"Do you ever move from that window?" Clara asked him.

Lassiter had already turned. Now he took a few steps toward her and smiled.

"There's not much to look at in here," he told her. "And I don't get many visitors."

Clara turned to Lund, who was eyeing Lassiter. "Can I have the lantern?" she asked.

Lund's eyebrows raised, but he finally handed it to her.

"You can go now, Marshal," she said. "I'll come out front when I'm ready."

Lund reluctantly turned and left Clara alone with Lassiter. Both Clara and Lassiter waited until he had gotten clear back to his desk before they began their conversation. It was Clara who spoke first.

"I suppose you're wondering what brings me here to see you. I'll make it short and simple. I don't believe you killed Allen. I think someone else did. But I'm not sure about what you told my father this afternoon—I'm not sure about Hardy Malone."

"You can be sure about him," Lassiter said. "I don't know all the reasons, but you can be sure it was Malone who killed your fiancé."

Clara had by now pretty much cried herself dry over the death of her fiancé. Hearing the details of Allen Hutton's death wasn't going to make her mourn him any more than she already had. She had now become filled with anger over the murder, and wanted to know from Lassiter just what had happened.

Lassiter told her about his arrival at Porter Draw, explained to her the reason he had come to Cheyenne and his discussion with Allen Hutton just before Hutton was shot. Then he told her the circumstances of Hardy Malone and the Box Y cowhands showing up shortly after the shooting, and how Malone had tried so hard to have him lynched right away.

"I'm sure Malone was the man in the trees, who I ran off just after the shooting," Lassiter said. "But he's got me in a real fix here, and your town marshal isn't helping matters at all."

"Frankly, I would be more apt to consider Frank Lund as the man who shot Allen than Malone," Clara said. "That might sound a bit rash, but that's the way I feel."

"I happen to know Lund myself," Lassiter said. "He was a crook as a deputy marshal down in Abilene some years back, and I doubt if he's changed his ways."

Clara listened intently as Lassiter, speaking low, told her about Abilene and the bank robbery, and his gunfight with the three gamblers. Clara nodded through the story, as if not surprised at anything she was hearing.

"What has made you so suspicious of Lund?" Lassiter asked.

"I know all towns have their politics," Clara said. "But Lund is so obvious about catering to the men with the biggest bankrolls. I wouldn't put anything past him.''

Lassiter knew he was stepping on fragile ground by bringing Clara's father into it, but it had to be done.

"Why does your father think so highly of Lund?" Lassiter asked. "He immediately took Lund's word over mine."

"Don't misunderstand my father," Clara said quickly. "He can be a harsh man at times. But he's always fair. He's just very angry at seeing Allen killed in cold blood."

"It seems to me that he's marked me as guilty, though," Lassiter said.

"That's because you mentioned that you had intended to go to work for Jack Stanford," Clara said. "Jack Stanford has a bad name around here."

"Don't you think Hardy Malone might have something to do with that as well?" Lassiter asked her.

Clara thought about it. "That's always possible," she said. "You're going to have a hard time convincing even *me* that Jack Stanford isn't a thief. But I'll listen."

7

"JACK STANFORD IS AS good a man as you'll ever run into," Lassiter told Clara, in defense of his friend. "I don't know what's happened around here, but when I knew him, you could trust your life with him. And I did just that, more than once."

Clara nodded and studied Lassiter through the bars. The lantern light fickered, and she could see that his solemn face showed more than just a trace of anger. She could see that his allegiance for Jack Stanford was born of some kind of honor formed in years past. She could see that the honor was real.

"You really think that much of him?" she asked Lassiter.

"I do," he replied with a nod. "What did he do to get such a bad reputation with your father?"

"You know very well," Clara said. "You heard my father say that he's a thief."

"I can't believe that," Lassiter said. "Who's calling him a thief—your father?"

"Not just my father," Clara said quickly. "There are a lot of men in this valley feel the same way."

"But who started it all?" Lassiter asked. "Your father?"

"Why are you attacking my father?" she asked.

"I'm not, Clara," Lassiter said. "I'm just trying to get to the bottom of this. Did Jack do something to your father to make him feel that way? What happened? I need to know."

Clara lowered her head. Lassiter could see that she felt guilty about something; without a doubt, about Jack Stanford.

"I realize your father thinks Jack was a thief," Lassiter told her. "I heard him say it. But I haven't heard you say it yet."

Clara looked up and into Lassiter's eyes. She took a deep breath. "I guess I don't know what to believe about him," she finally said.

"Are you going to tell me how this rumor got started?" Lassiter asked.

"Maybe I'm as much to blame for his reputation as anybody," Clara admitted. "Maybe it isn't fair."

"Did something happen between you two?" Lassiter asked. He realized Clara's beauty would tempt any man, especially in a valley where few women lived.

Clara looked to one side and toyed with her purse. There was something within her that she was having trouble getting out.

"I'll bet Jack wanted to court you," Lassiter finally said. "Isn't that it?"

"I guess he came on to me pretty strong at first, and I didn't like that," Clara replied with a nod. "He just isn't my type. And when Allen came along, he and Allen got into a couple of fights." She stopped talking and continued to fiddle with her purse.

"Why would that be enough to give him a bad reputation?" Lassiter asked.

"There's a lot more to the story," Clara finally continued. "Jack just wouldn't take no for an answer. Then Allen caught him with some of our horses."

"What do you mean he caught him with some of your horses?" Lassiter asked. "You mean he was taking them?"

"I don't know if he was or not," Clara replied. "We just heard Allen's side of the story—that he caught Jack taking them. Jack swears up and down he was just bringing them back to our ranch, so they wouldn't stray too far away."

"And you all chose not to believe Jack, is that it?" Lassiter asked.

"I wasn't there. But according to Allen, he was driving them in the wrong direction to be taking them to our ranch. We all believed Allen. I didn't know for certain about the whole thing, but I certainly wanted Jack Stanford to know that I wasn't interested in him. That seemed to be the easiest way to make him back down."

"So, what do you really feel?" Lassiter asked her.

"I don't know."

"You must have some feeling."

"I said I don't know."

Lassiter took a deep breath. "How many horses did your fiancé catch Jack with?" Lassiter asked.

"Two."

"Just two?"

"Just two."

"How could anybody make it worth his time to steal just two horses?" Lassiter asked.

"You have a point," Clara admitted. "There were

ten others just over the hill. I suppose, had he been stealing, he would have taken them as well.''

"That would make more sense than just taking two and leaving the others,'' Lassiter said with a nod. "But now the story is around that he's prone to stealing, and he can't prove otherwise to anyone. That will make it hard for him to be able to stay in this area, don't you think?''

"I suppose so,'' Clara answered. "I guess that's what I wanted to happen.''

Lassiter began to think aloud then. "I'm surprised Malone didn't kill your fiancé earlier and pin it on Jack. Or maybe that was the original idea.''

Clara looked hard at Lassiter. "You have no doubt at all that Hardy Malone killed Allen, do you? How can you be so very certain?''

"I've explained all that,'' Lassiter said. "The way things happened today, and Hardy Malone's attitude, have convinced me he did the killing. But no one wants to listen to me. It seems everyone around here has their minds made up.''

Clara could detect the anger in Lassiter's tone. She couldn't blame him—he had come into a valley to see an old friend and now found himself set to be hanged, just as soon as a judge declared him guilty. And his friend, Jack Stanford, could easily find himself in the same situation.

"How do you intend to prove your innocence, and Malone's guilt?'' Clara asked.

"There's not much I can do by myself,'' Lassiter said. "Not when no one wants to hear anything I've got to say.''

"Maybe there is something I can do to delay the trial,'' Clara suggested.

"If you could convince your father that I didn't kill

your fiancé, that would make things a whole lot easier," Lassiter said. "I'm sure he respects your opinion."

Clara thought for a time. She was even more certain now that Lassiter hadn't committed the crime. She could understand how Lassiter would insist that Malone was the killer, since Malone had come on the scene so quickly and wanted to hang Lassiter right away. But Clara didn't think Lassiter was necessarily right; he didn't know Malone that well.

Clara knew that Malone was prone to recklessness and hasty decisions. That was one of the reasons her father had decided not to hire him. Malone had asked for work any number of times, but his personality was too volatile.

After thinking about it more, Clara felt that Malone had wanted to make a big thing of Allen's killing, more to impress her father than anything else. She was of the opinion that Malone would feel he had a better chance to go to work for the Box Y if he was the one to bring Allen Hutton's killer to justice. He would do almost anything to get close to her father.

Another thought then occurred to her. Jack Stanford. He would have a lot of reasons for killing Allen, especially since Allen was engaged to her.

The anger of losing her fiancé returned to her. Clara now began to think that maybe Jack Stanford was the killer. She looked hard at Lassiter through the bars.

"What's the matter?" he asked her.

"You sure do seem to be on Jack Stanford's side in all this," she told him. "What makes you so sure *he* didn't kill Allen?"

Lassiter was taken aback. "That doesn't sound like the Jack Stanford I know," he said. "If he wanted to kill somebody, he wouldn't shoot them in the back. He's not afraid to come straight on, to anybody."

"Where is Jack Stanford now?" Clara asked. "He hasn't been in to see you yet, has he?"

"No, he hasn't," Lassiter told her. "I've been wondering that myself. Surely everyone for miles around knows about me being in this jail by now."

"Maybe you'd better think again about your good friend, Jack Stanford," Clara said. "Maybe you had better reconsider and wonder if it wasn't him after all."

Lassiter was silent while Clara walked back to the front of the jail and set the lantern down on Lund's desk. Lund got up, blew the lantern out, and followed Clara into the street.

Lassiter walked back over to the window and peered through darkness. Clara was on her horse, riding out of town, and Lund was talking to someone in the street. Lassiter could hear Lund's voice; he was talking about Jack Stanford.

Jack Stanford drove five head of horses ahead of him. He had just bought them, and they were freshly branded. Now no one could say Jack Stanford needed horses and had taken to stealing them from neighboring ranches.

He was just finishing the ride back down to Cheyenne from the headwaters country of Powder River. He had heard there was good horseflesh in that country, and had decided to bolster his stock. He expected to expand his herd of longhorns, and needed extra horses for the men he intended to hire before long.

Stanford had been going the better part of a week and was glad to be back, but the glow of light from the Cheyenne saloons gave him mixed feelings.

There would be those who would be glad to see him back and those who wouldn't. Especially when word reached the bigger ranchers, who wouldn't be happy that he was still planning to stick it out in the valley.

He wondered if the rumors that had followed him all summer had become worse, and if anyone at all wanted him to stay. He had managed to convince Trace McCord—for the time being, anyway—that he had not tried to steal two Box Y horses earlier in the spring. McCord had listened to Allen Hutton's side and then to his. For some reason, McCord had decided there wasn't clear evidence of rustling and had not pushed the matter.

But Stanford knew that McCord had ideas that he had been rustling. But McCord was a man who didn't act hastily, and he was respected in the valley. For that Stanford was grateful.

But not everyone had been ready to drop it so quickly. There were a lot of cattlemen in the valley already, almost too many. And with more coming in, there was keen competition for space and grass for cattle herds. The big ranchers were already banding together to keep the competition from smaller settlers down. The smaller ones were going to be squeezed out before long.

For that reason, Jack Stanford had decided he was going to be one of those who stayed. It wouldn't be easy, but he would make it.

The upcoming Fourth of July horse race was going to make somebody a lot of money. Stanford felt that winning that race would ensure his position in the valley.

That was the reason he had sent for his long time friend. Lassiter's big black stallion could run as well over a short or long distance, either one, as any horse born. The stallion had been born with pure endurance. If anyone could win the race, Lassiter could.

But now Jack Stanford worried. He was certain his old friend would have arrived by now. Stanford wasn't certain how long Lassiter would stick around if he couldn't find him right away, and he worried that he might have already come and gone. The only way he would be able to know was to ask in town.

Stanford hadn't told anyone where he had gone nor how long he had intended to be away. There was no one he could trust, no way to tell who would want him to come back with five good horses and who wouldn't.

He stopped outside of Cheyenne at his ranch head-quarters and corralled his horses. He didn't worry about them, as nobody even knew he was gone. Now he would ride into town and catch up on what had happened while he was out of the valley.

It was well past dark when he got into Cheyenne. The town seemed somehow disquieted, and there were those who stared hard at him as he tied his horse to one of the many railings along the main street. Once he reached a saloon for a drink, it didn't take him long to realize that something big had happened while he was gone.

After overhearing a number of conversations, Stanford asked the bartender what all the commotion was about. He promptly learned that a stranger dressed in black had killed Allen Hutton at a stream crossing just outside town. The stranger was now in jail, awaiting trial.

"Is this stranger's name Lassiter?" Stanford asked the bartender.

"That's his name, all right," the bartender said. "And word has it he came to work for you."

The way the bartender said it led Stanford to feel that he was being accused as well. That feeling grew stronger when he turned to see Frank Lund standing beside him, his gun drawn.

"I've been expecting you," Lund said. "Let's take a trip over to the jail."

8

STANFORD STOOD STILL WHILE Lund stuck the barrel of his revolver into his ribs.

"You heard me," Lund said gruffly. "We're going to jail. Let's have your pistol—slowly."

Stanford looked all around him. Everyone in the saloon was staring. It seemed as if they were all ready to draw and fire, to make sure there was no attempt at escape.

"What's this all about?" Stanford asked.

"Don't act so innocent," Lund said. "You're under arrest for conspiracy to commit murder."

"That's ridiculous," Stanford said angrily, handing his pistol to Lund.

With one quick motion Lund slammed his pistol into Jack Stanford's skull. Stanford's hat cushioned the blow, but his knees buckled and he held onto the bar as long as he could before he slumped to the floor.

The ceiling was spinning. He could feel Lund's hand jerking on his upper arm.

"Get up, Stanford. I didn't hit you that hard."

Lund jerked Stanford to his knees. He wobbled there for a time before making it to his feet. Then he fell again.

"Get up!" Lund yelled.

Stanford felt Lund's boot smashing into his ribs. He curled sideways as Lund prepared for another kick.

"You ain't going to get him to jail that way, Lund," came a voice from among the onlookers.

Everyone turned to see Johnny Ridge shoulder his way to the front of the crowd. He was staring hard at Lund.

"What the hell do you think you're doing, butting in?" Lund asked.

"That man owes me a horse," Johnny said. "I want him alive, so I can collect my debt."

There was silence in the saloon. Everyone now stared at Johnny Ridge. Brazen was more than an apt description for this young cowboy.

"He was supposed to be getting some horses for his spread," Johnny continued. "If you kill him, how am I supposed to collect what's due me?"

Lund was still dumbfounded. He could see that Ridge was challenging him, but could really do nothing about it. He couldn't go over and just pistol-whip him as he had Stanford. Ridge hadn't put himself into a position where he looked like an outlaw.

"You may never get your horse," Lund finally said. "This man conspired with that gunfighter to kill Allen Hutton. It's likely he'll hang on the Fourth of July right beside Lassiter."

Stanford was pulling himself to his feet now, steadying himself against the bar. His head was bowed and he shook it repeatedly, trying to erase the pain and the cobwebs.

Johnny looked at Stanford and then back to Lund.

"You say he was behind Allen Hutton's death?" Johnny asked Lund.

Lund nodded. "There's reason to believe that."

"There's reason," Johnny said, "but is there any proof?"

Lund glared at Johnny. "We'll have enough proof when the time comes."

"In the meantime, you just do what you want with him—is that it?" Johnny demanded. "What kind of law is that?"

"Ridge, you're on thin ice," Lund said. He took a step toward Johnny.

Johnny shook his head, as if he couldn't believe it. He turned to the crowd.

"How would you like to be treated like this, and maybe be innocent?" he asked. "Think about it. Some big cattleman like Trace McCord gets his sights set on you and that gives Lund, here, a license to beat you over the head with a pistol. And then put you behind bars so you can look forward to hanging. Doesn't seem like justice to me."

The crowd started to talk among themselves. Johnny didn't stop there, but called the other hand who knew about Malone forward. When Curly was beside him, Johnny continued.

"Some of you heard me say before that Hardy Malone had reason to kill Allen Hutton. Curly, here, knows for certain that Malone was gunning for Hutton because of a brother of his Hutton supposedly killed at Shiloh during the war."

"All that's hearsay," Frank said.

Lund was obviously very nervous. He was looking hard at Johnny. The crowd was talking among themselves even more now.

"If you know what's good for you, Ridge, you and

Curly will head back to the Box Y right now and hope you have a job tomorrow," Lund warned.

"My job's not in jeopardy," Johnny said.

"Don't be so sure," Lund said. "It sounded to me like you were trying to make Trace McCord look bad." He looked among the men in the saloon. "Didn't you all see it that way?"

Some nodded and some didn't. There was a division. Johnny had gotten some of them to thinking. Lund then turned back to Johnny.

"I'll see that Trace McCord hears about this," he added. "We'll see if he likes the idea of you trying to make him look bad. I'll bet you're out of this valley before the next sundown."

Lund took Jack Stanford roughly by the arm and escorted him past Johnny and the others toward the door of the saloon. Just before going out, Lund turned to look hard at Johnny, then elbowed his way with Stanford through the batwing doors, leaving them swinging wildly.

It was well after nightfall when Johnny Ridge and Curly got back to the Box Y. The moon was nearly full, and in a cloudless sky, it bathed the land in a mantle of white light.

Johnny had decided it was important to tell Trace McCord his concerns about Hardy Malone. There was no doubt in his mind that Malone represented a threat to everybody who didn't think like he did. Johnny was certain there would be a lot of trouble to come if Malone wasn't seen for the man he really was.

What's more, Johnny didn't consider it fair that the stranger locked up in Frank Lund's jail was going to stand trial and likely hang for a crime that Malone committed. Johnny hoped this visit with McCord would make a difference.

When they entered the ranch yard, Johnny noticed Clara's horse was not in the corral. Trace McCord's roan was in with the big red stallion, standing lazily in the night air, but there was no sign of Clara's horse anywhere.

"Let's go in and talk to McCord right away," Johnny suggested.

"You go ahead, and I'll wait at the bunkhouse," Curly said. "I want to find some money and go back into town. I feel lucky tonight, and the keno tables are hot."

Curly rode over to the bunkhouse and left his horse outside, with the reins down. Johnny didn't care about going back into town, and so he rode straight to the ranch house. He tied his horse to the hitching post out front, thinking about what he was going to tell Trace McCord and how he was going to say it.

He had just started up the walkway to the house when he noticed another rider come into the yard.

There was plenty of moonlight, but the lone rider was a distance away and it was too dark to see him clearly. The rider appeared to be restraining his horse, looking around the place. But something deep within Johnny told him for certain that the rider was Hardy Malone.

He saw Malone turn his horse for the bunkhouse just as Trace McCord opened the door to the ranch house, holding a lantern in his hand.

"Johnny, something I can do for you?" he asked.

Johnny turned back to answer McCord. Malone had just dismounted in the darkness in front of the bunkhouse and was going in.

"Yes, I wanted to talk to you, if I could," Johnny said nervously.

"Sure. Come on in."

McCord held the door while Johnny removed his hat and walked past him into the house.

"Did you just come from town?" McCord asked, setting the lantern on a table.

Johnny nodded.

"Did you see Clara there?"

"I didn't," Johnny replied. "But I guess I wasn't looking for her. She could have been there and I just didn't notice her horse."

McCord nodded. He was looking out the window toward the trail that came down the hill into the ranch yard.

"I should go into town and look for her," McCord said.

"This won't take long, McCord," Johnny said, fumbling with his hat. "I wouldn't trouble you, but I think it's awful important."

"You must," McCord agreed, turning from the window. "You've never been up here to the house to talk to me before. Have a seat."

Johnny looked around the spacious living room, noting the oak and chestnut decor. Much of the furniture had been shipped from the East and was as beautiful as Johnny had ever seen anywhere. But he was too nervous to sit down.

"I'll just tell you and be gone," Johnny said.

"What is it, Johnny?" McCord asked. "What's troubling you?"

"It's Hardy Malone. I think he's a killer." Johnny said it quickly and without hesitation. "I really think it was Malone who killed Allen, not that stranger in the jail."

Johnny noted that McCord was studying him hard. It was obvious that McCord had heard this about Malone before and had been wondering. Now that he was hearing it again, it was making him wonder even more.

"What makes you say that, Johnny?" McCord asked.

"I know about Allen killing Malone's brother in the war," Johnny said. "I don't know how many others know about it, but I think that's why Malone would shoot Allen."

Johnny went on to relate the story he had heard from Curly about the war and Malone's talk about squaring the score with Allen Hutton. McCord admitted that he hadn't heard that and could see that might provoke someone like Malone into shooting someone.

"I saw him just ride up," Johnny then said. "Why don't we find out if it's true about the war?"

"You saw Malone ride up?" McCord said. "Are you sure?"

"It was him," Johnny said. "I know it was."

"What would he be doing here now?" McCord wondered aloud. He grabbed the lantern on the table once again and then his hat. Then he strode quickly out of the house ahead of Johnny.

"I don't know what all is going on," McCord said in a gruff tone as they walked, "but all this is starting to get on my nerves. A lot is happening awfully fast here." He was looking out toward the hills where he hoped Clara would come riding back into the ranch yard.

Johnny followed McCord through the darkness and began to get nervous, for there was no longer any lantern light in the bunkhouse. The closer they got, the more Johnny was certain that there were no longer any horses out in front either.

"What were you saying about Malone being here?" McCord finally asked. "I don't see that *anyone* is here."

"Malone was here," Johnny said defensively. "I saw him ride up. And Curly rode over here while I was going in to talk to you. I wonder what's going on here."

"I don't know," McCord said. "I don't understand any of this."

The sound of another rider could be heard, and finally Clara rode her horse into the ranch yard. McCord momentarily forgot about Malone and Curly and ran to the house to greet her. Johnny hurried along behind him.

"Clara, where have you been, for God's sake?" McCord asked his daughter.

"I wanted to get some things straight in my mind," Clara said, dismounting. "But I'm not certain I know any more now than I did before about this whole thing."

"Were you in talking to that stranger?" McCord asked.

Clara nodded as she walked into the house, followed by her father and Johnny. "I'm certain that he didn't do the shooting. But I'm not sure about Malone, or anybody else for that matter. It occurred to me that Jack Stanford possibly has some connection to all of this."

"No, not Jack Stanford," Johnny spoke up. "He's not that kind."

They were in the front hall now. Both Clara and her father were facing Johnny now, and he was as sincere as he knew how to be.

"Stanford doesn't work that way," Johnny continued. "I know he likes you a great deal, Clara, but he's just too proud a man to do anything underhanded just because he lost out to Allen."

"Be careful of your talk," McCord told Johnny.

"I don't mean no harm, McCord," Johnny said. "I just think we'd ought to think about Malone. I'm afraid he's taken Curly somewhere now."

"Why wouldn't we have heard them leave?" McCord asked.

"Malone knows this country," Johnny said. "He could have got the drop on Curly and took him out the back way, into the hills behind the ranch. I know for a fact he's gunning for both Curly and me, ever since today."

McCord asked Johnny what had happened, and Johnny explained the incidents with Malone and then Frank Lund, as he was arresting Jack Stanford. McCord tried to tell Johnny that maybe he was overreacting and that possibly Curly had gone back into town with the rider, who could have been just one of the hands.

"I don't think so," Johnny said, turning for the door. "I thank you for your time. I think I'll go back into town now and see if I can learn anything more."

He left McCord and Clara and got quickly on his horse. He knew there was something terribly wrong now, and he had to find out what had happened to Curly, fast. His own life depended on it.

9

LASSITER STOOD AT THE BACK of the cell, where Lund had ordered him, and watched the cell door swing back. Jack Stanford fell forward and to the floor after Lund gave him a hard push.

Stanford was battered and beaten. Since taking him from the saloon, Lund had hauled him into an alley to try and get a confession out of him. But Stanford had refused to admit to something he knew nothing about.

As Jack Stanford fell forward, Lassiter thought seriously of trying to get to Lund. But Lund was obviously furious about something and would no doubt use his pistol in an instant if provoked. It almost appeared as if he wanted to kill somebody anyway, no matter who it might be.

"There's your partner, Lassiter," Lund slurred. "You'll hang together."

Lund slammed the cell door shut and went back to his desk. He tossed the keys back down on the desk, blew out the lantern, and left the jail.

Lassiter helped his friend to a reclining position on the one beaten cot within the cell.

"Jack, what happened?"

Stanford was groggy. He was in obvious pain and had trouble speaking. But he wanted to tell Lassiter what had occurred.

"It seems like I'm being pulled in on a killing that happened this afternoon," Stanford managed. "You kill Allen Hutton?"

"No," Lassiter replied. He studied Stanford in the light of the moon that shone through the window bars. He concluded that Stanford was in no condition for stressful questions, and decided everything could wait until morning.

He was trying to get his friend as comfortable as he could on the bunk when he heard someone at the window.

"Lassiter. I have to talk to you."

It was Johnny Ridge, peering through the cell window bars, his face silhouetted with the moon behind him.

Lassiter hurried over and found Johnny nervous, breathing as if he had come in a great hurry.

"You're putting yourself in a lot of danger," Lassiter told him. "What if somebody should see you?"

"I'll take my chances," Johnny said. "If I don't get some help with Hardy Malone, he'll see to it that I'm dead also."

"What do you mean?" Lassiter asked.

"I can't find Curly anywhere," Johnny explained. "I was out to tell Trace McCord about Malone, and he showed up while I was talking to McCord. I know he took Curly somewhere and killed him. I just know it."

"What's this all about?" Lassiter asked.

"I know that Hardy Malone had a reason to kill

Allen Hutton, a reason that's more than the race or anything else," Johnny replied. "Allen Hutton killed Malone's brother at the battle of Shiloh. He's been tracking Hutton ever since."

Lassiter was interested in the news. It certainly seemed like Malone had taken a crazy chance in shooting Hutton in the back right before his eyes. But when there's a blood feud going on, logic and reason usually fall to blind emotion—in this case, hatred on the part of Hardy Malone.

"How did you find this out?" Lassiter asked.

"There's another cowhand that I ride with a lot," Johnny explained, "this Curly I mentioned before. That's all anybody knows him by."

"Was he the cowhand at the draw, who went to town with you?"

"Yes, that was Curly. Anyway, Curly told me he recognized Malone when he came into the valley. It seems Curly heard him talking in a saloon in Denver last year sometime. But Curly's the only one who heard him say it, and he told me this afternoon. When we were in town, we found Malone in a saloon, and we told everyone in the saloon. Maybe some of them believed us, I don't know."

"If you told a lot of people, then what are you worried about?" Lassiter asked. "Malone would be a fool to kill either of you now. Everyone would be suspicious."

"You don't know Malone very well, do you?" Johnny said. "I think he already killed Curly."

"What makes you think that?" Lassiter asked.

"Because I haven't see Curly since I went out to the ranch and told McCord tonight. Curly was in the bunkhouse, and I saw Malone ride in. When I got done talking to Trace McCord, neither Curly nor Malone were around. I came into town, and I can't find either one of them."

"I'm not in much of a position to do you much good," Lassiter said. "Everybody wants to hang me. What kind of help can I give you?"

"If I can bust you and Jack Stanford out of here, we can get Malone together," Johnny said. "But I don't have a chance out here alone, and you two don't have a chance in there."

"They would think we were guilty for sure if we broke out," Lassiter pointed out. "And if you got involved yourself, Frank Lund would do what he could to see you hang along with us."

"I'm involved anyway," Johnny argued. "Malone is out to get me, and Frank Lund won't care one way or the other. He's got you two. He's happy."

Lassiter could see Johnny's point. Frank Lund wasn't apt to care much at all about what happened to anybody, just so his prisoners were locked up and ready to hang when the time came. As far as Lund was concerned, the case was closed.

"What should I do?" Johnny asked Lassiter. "How can I stay alive?"

"Stick close to McCord," Lassiter suggested. "Make sure you're never alone around Malone."

"That's easier said than done," Johnny said. "How can I work like I'm supposed to? How—"

Johnny's question was broken off by a yell from Frank Lund, who was crossing the street from one of the saloons.

"Who's there?" he shouted. "Stay where you are!"

Johnny bolted from the window and ran into the shadows. Lund continued to yell. Lassiter jumped back from the window as Lund suddenly opened fire, sending bullets everywhere in the vicinity of the cell window.

Lund shot a number of times, bringing people into the street from all directions. Lassiter watched and listened from the cell window as the town came alive and everyone hunted through the streets and alleys for Johnny Ridge.

But Lassiter wasn't sure that any of them knew who they were looking for. Not once in all the yelling and shouting did he hear anyone mention Johnny's name. They were just looking for someone who had run away from the window of the jail and into the shadows.

Jack Stanford tried to rise to his feet, but his strength was gone and he collapsed. Lassiter helped him back onto the bunk and told him to stay there no matter what happened or he might injure himself more or even cause his own death.

After a time Lund came into the jail with some other men. He was brandishing a lantern, and held it up to the bars of the cell.

"Who was at the window, Lassiter?" Lund demanded.

"Don't you know?" Lassiter asked.

"I wouldn't be asking you if I did, now would I?" Lund said sarcastically.

Lassiter responded with an equal edge to his voice. "You shot at him, Lund. Do you make a habit of shooting at people before you know who they are or what they're doing?"

"Don't be smart with me, Lassiter," Lund said. "You either tell me who was at the window or I'll come in there and get it out of you."

Lund felt confident with a number of the townsmen and local cowhands behind him. He was going to show everyone who was boss.

"Are you going to tell me?" Lund asked Lassiter again. "Or do I have to come in there?"

"Come on in, Lund," Lassiter challenged. "I would welcome that, and I'd treat you real special."

Lund was held silent a moment by the icy tone of Lassiter's voice. But he was dealt the hand, and now he was going to have to play the cards. Once again, he had put himself in the position of saving face.

Lund turned to one of the men. "Hold this lantern. And shoot him if he tries to escape. I'm going to teach him a lesson."

Lassiter waited patiently while Lund turned the key in the cell-door lock. Lassiter put his hand on Jack Stanford and told him to just stay put. Lund then pulled the iron-barred door back and came toward Lassiter, his pistol raised. As he neared Lassiter, he brought the pistol down in an arc.

Lassiter had no trouble blocking Lund's forward motion. With his free hand, Lassiter landed a heavy blow with his fist into Lund's midsection, doubling him over. Lund's breath went out in a whoosh and he gasped. Lassiter then pulled him up by the hair and landed a savage blow to his face, knocking him backward, through the cell door.

There was the roar of gunfire, and Lassiter moved instantly to one side as one of the men shot into the cell. The bullet whined off a bar in the cell window. The man was thumbing back the hammer for another shot when a loud voice filled the room.

"What the hell is going on here?"

Trace McCord pushed his way through the men and jerked the pistol out of the man's hand. He shoved the man backward, causing him to nearly fall over.

"I asked what the hell you men are doing!" he yelled again.

Lund was just coming to his knees, still unable to speak. Some of the men stammered that Lassiter was trying to escape. McCord, infuriated, called them all liars.

"I told you this was going to be done the legal way," McCord roared, his voice booming in the closed quarters. "You don't listen, do you? Not any of you."

McCord watched while the men backed away from him. A few of them even left. Then he turned to Frank Lund, who was rising to his feet, trying to recover from the blows Lassiter had dealt him.

"Lund, what is this all about?" McCord asked. "And it better be good."

"Someone was at the cell window, Trace," Lund blurted. "He was planning to break this gunfighter out of jail. We just tried to stop it, that's all."

Lund looked aorund. "So where's the man that was at the cell window?"

Lund wiped blood from his lips. His mouth was already starting to swell badly.

"He got away," Lund finally managed.

McCord stared hard at Lund. "Who was he?"

Lund shrugged.

"What are you doing in here, then? Why aren't you out after him?"

"We were looking for him," Lund managed. "But he got away."

"And you thought you could get Lassiter to tell you who it was, is that it?" McCord guessed correctly.

Lund nodded. "But he won't tell."

"How could you expect him to?" McCord asked. "That's foolish." He looked again at the man who had fired the shot at Lassiter. "I don't like any of this even a little bit," he added. "If this man had been killed . . ."

Everyone sensed that McCord's anger was rising even more now. They all backed away a few more steps.

"How do you expect a judge to even bring the case to trial if you do this kind of thing?" McCord asked the group. "If word of this got into a courtroom, they'd throw the case out in a minute."

No one spoke. The air was heavy with McCord's anger. It was all he could do to keep from hitting one of them. Finally, he turned on Frank Lund.

"I've been hearing things about you, Lund," he said. "Stories about how you ran things in Abilene as a deputy. It looks to me like you haven't got the sense you were born with. Next time something like this happens, you'll be looking for another job. You got that?"

Lund, his head lowered, nodded. He shuffled past McCord, who stood glowering with his hands on his hips. The other men were already filing out of the jail. Lund managed to get to his desk and sit down. He remained doubled over for a time, fighting against the pain from Lassiter's blows.

McCord remained standing at the entrance to the cell. The door was still open. He walked in, unafraid of Lassiter, and looked down at Jack Stanford.

"How bad is he hurt?" McCord asked.

"He needs a doctor," Lassiter answered. "Lund pistol-whipped him pretty bad."

McCord looked at Stanford. "He'll be fine."

"Yeah, at least he won't be after your daughter, will he?" Lassiter said.

McCord's face turned hard. "You don't like me, do you?"

"Any reason I should?" Lassiter asked. "You're ready to see me hang."

"I just want Allen Hutton's killer, is all," McCord said.

"Then listen to me," Lassiter said. "So far you haven't cared to hear me out."

McCord shook his head. "I don't get all of this," he said. "What is blowing up all of a sudden here? There's got to be more to this than just the upcoming horse race."

"I tried to tell you that earlier," Lassiter said. "And now I'm even more convinced that Hardy Malone is behind it all."

McCord studied Lassiter closely. "Was the man at the window by any chance Johnny Ridge?"

Lassiter knew that McCord wasn't going to go after Johnny. And even if he was, nobody had caught Johnny. What's more, there hadn't been any crime committed.

"Was it?" McCord asked again.

Lassiter nodded. "He's worried about his friend Curly. I don't blame him."

"He talked to me tonight about that," McCord acknowledged. "And I understood my daughter spoke to you. I don't like that."

"She came here," Lassiter said. "Maybe you had better talk to her about it."

"All I'm saying is, don't try and manipulate her feelings," McCord told Lassiter. "She's upset enough as it is. The funeral is tomorrow, and she's not looking forward to it."

"I'm sorry about what's happened," Lassiter said. "But I'm not to blame. Hardy Malone is."

"But the evidence points to you," McCord said. "That's what Frank Lund says."

"Why do you think Hardy Malone is innocent of all this?" Lassiter asked him.

"I don't know if he is," McCord replied. "But I have to go by what the marshal says. I have to have some faith in him. Otherwise, he isn't much good, is he?"

"You said it, I didn't," Lassiter told McCord. "You couldn't have done much worse."

McCord grunted. "It really doesn't matter at this point. What's important is what happens during your trial. A jury will decide whether you're innocent or guilty."

"I believe that's already been decided," Lassiter said. There was no irritation in his tone, just a sense of fact. "But that doesn't mean I'll hang."

McCord studied Lassiter for a time. Finally, he walked out and closed the cell door.

"I'm not sure now if you killed Allen or not," he said through the bars. "It's too bad that things turned out the way they did—I mean, with you being there when Allen was shot, and all. Under different circumstances, I would give you Lund's job and send him packing."

"No, you wouldn't give me Lund's job," Lassiter said. "I wouldn't have it. I don't do other people's dirty work."

McCord grunted again. "Well, it doesn't matter. The judge will be here in two days. After that, you won't have to worry about any kind of work ever again."

McCord turned and stomped out of the building, passing Frank Lund without even acknowledging his presence. Lund was left rubbing blood from his broken lips by the light of the lantern. Lassiter stood in his cell and watched for a time, while Stanford tried to rest on the bunk.

"We've got to do it," Stanford said from the bunk.

"We've got to get out of here. They'll hang us both for sure."

"You're in no condition to talk about breaking out of jail," Lassiter said.

"I'm better off than if I had a noose around my neck," Stanford remarked. "That makes you permanently ill."

Lassiter nodded. "You've got a point."

"Didn't McCord say the funeral was tomorrow?" Stanford asked.

"That's right," Lassiter said. "That may be our only chance to get out of this town without having a whole lot of people after us right away."

Stanford laid back down. "I've got an idea," he finally said. "I know Frank Lund better than you do. There's a way we can get out of here and make him look like a fool. Would that suit you?"

Lassiter was looking from the window into the street. The town had pretty much quieted down for the night. He nodded.

"Tomorrow is the last day I ever want to see that man again," Lassiter said. "Ever again."

10

LASSITER SLEPT FRETFULLY sitting down in one corner of the cell. Jack Stanford fared no better on the cot. His head still ached from the pistol-whipping, and his ribs were sore from the pounding Lund had given him.

But when dawn broke into the sky, both men were ready to enact their plan.

Stanford laid back in the bunk and allowed Lassiter to pull the old blanket completely up over his head. When Frank Lund arrived to check on them, he noticed Lassiter standing over the cot, his head bowed.

Lund was dressed in a black suit and vest for the funeral. His mind was on the events of the morning and not on the possibility that something had happened to Jack Stanford.

"What's going on in there?" Lund asked.

"He's died," Lassiter told Lund without looking up. "You've killed him."

"What?" Lund was startled. He brought the keys and came to the door. "What? I never killed him."

"You'll have some explaining to do to McCord," Lassiter said. "You had better figure out a good story."

"You two must have gotten into a fight," Lund said, obviously startled. "He wasn't anywhere near dying when I put him in there."

"Maybe you didn't look at him close enough," Lassiter suggested.

Lund pulled his pistol and unlocked the cell door. He moved in quickly, motioning Lassiter to the back of the cell. Lassiter moved back calmly, but eyeing Lund with a hint of anger—just enough to make Lund believe that Stanford was actually dead.

Lund kicked the bunk once. There was no response from Stanford. Lund edged closer to the bunk, watching Lassiter from the corner of his eye. Then Lund turned his eyes directly on the bunk.

Lassiter waited. Lund was staring at Stanford's still form with the blanket over the prisoner's face. Lund didn't want to believe that Stanford was actually dead, but it certainly appeared that way.

Finally, he leaned over to remove the blanket, and Stanford rose up in the bunk and yelled.

Lund shouted and jumped back to get away, and Lassiter grabbed his gun while he was off balance. Lund had no chance to resist, as he was terrified from the shock of seeing Stanford rise up in the bunk. But he wasn't going to let Lassiter get the drop on him if he could help it, and lunged forward.

Lassiter had little patience for Lund, and slammed Lund's own pistol into his head, dropping him to the floor like a stone.

"See how you like it," Lassiter said as Lund lay still in a heap.

"Hit him again," Stanford suggested.

"We don't want to kill him," Lassiter said. "Just knock him out of commission for a while."

Stanford noted the blood trickling from Lund's head. "You succeeded in doing that," he said. "But I'd just as soon finish him."

"That wouldn't be smart," Lassiter replied. "I know what he did to you in the alley, but killing him won't solve anything. We've got to get out of here."

Lassiter and Stanford then bound and gagged the unconscious Frank Lund and locked him in his own cell. Lassiter held onto the key chain.

"I'll throw these away when we get out of town," he said. "Lund will have plenty of time to get used to that cell."

"That was easier than I thought," Stanford said. "I wasn't sure he would fall for it."

"We're not out of here yet, not by a long shot," Lassiter reminded him. "The only thing we've got going for us is that everyone's over in the church."

Lassiter and Stanford hurried to Lund's desk. Lassiter tried the keys until he opened a drawer where Lund was keeping his pistols. Stanford's pistol was also there. Lassiter then went into the gun cabinet and took some extra ammunition from Lund's collection.

Jack Stanford gently strapped his own gun belt back on, then held his ribs. Lassiter tore a strip from a shirt of Lund's that was hanging nearby and wrapped Stanford's chest. Stanford let his breath out slowly. The wrapping was helping, but he was still in a great deal of pain.

"I hate to be such a cripple," he said.

"You think you can stay in a saddle?" Lassiter asked.

"Tie me in it if you have to," Stanford replied. Then

he asked, "What do you think we should do? Where will we go?"

"You know the land around here better than I do," Lassiter said. "After we find our horses at the livery stable, we'll get back into some rough country."

"You know they'll brand us both as killers for sure now, don't you?" Stanford said. "I'm not complaining, though. It's better than the alternative."

Lassiter found his rifle and made sure it was still in working order. After getting their hats and checking their pistols once again, the two men snuck from the jail. They followed the back alleys, hugging the corners of the buildings, until they reached the livery stables.

"Dammit!" Stanford hissed. "I was hoping nobody would be here."

There was a young boy feeding and grooming the horses. It was apparent he liked Lassiter's black stallion, for he was spending extra time petting his nose and feeding him oats from his open hand.

After some time thinking about what to do, Lassiter snuck up behind the boy and clamped a hand over his mouth. The terrified youth tried to squirm his way free. He finally slowed down when Lassiter assured him he wouldn't hurt him.

"I just want my horse, son," Lassiter said. "And my friend wants his horse. We don't mean you any harm. But we don't want you to yell either. Will you promise me you'll stay quiet?"

The boy nodded, and Lassiter released him. The boy turned, still afraid.

"You're the one who killed Allen Hutton," he said. "How did you get out of jail?"

Lassiter tried to get the boy to relax. "I don't know what you've heard about me, son," he said. "But I didn't do anyone in this valley any harm. All I want to do is get out of here with my friend and keep from being hanged.''

The boy looked at Lassiter wide-eyed for a few moments and then finally let himself relax. He seemed to understand that he didn't have anything to worry about from this man dressed in black. Despite what he had heard, this gunfighter seemed to be just an ordinary person.

''There's talk about what happened to Allen Hutton,'' the boy said. ''But you didn't shoot him?''

''I certainly didn't,'' Lassiter said. ''You stay right beside me while I saddle my horse.''

The boy wasn't over nine or ten years old. He was strong from the hard work he had no doubt been performing for a number of years already. And he seemed to be wise beyond his age to the ways of the world.

''Is there anyone else around here with you?'' Lassiter asked.

''No,'' the boy said. ''Pa and Uncle Jim are at the funeral. There's nobody around. Ain't you scared?''

Lassiter was throwing his saddle up on the stallion's back. He turned to the boy.

''You bet I am, son. I don't like the idea of being branded a killer. And it bothers me that this town is so sure of what happened out there in that draw the other day. It didn't happen like they think it did, and I can't change their minds. So my friend and I have to escape as fast as we can.''

Jack Stanford had his horse saddled and was anxious to get going. The boy noticed Stanford's face and the wrapping around his chest, and asked what had happened.

"The marshal got mad at him," Lassiter explained. "Nobody in this town likes either of us very well."

The boy stared at Lassiter's guns while Lassiter finished getting the stallion ready to ride.

"Those are big guns of yours," he said. "How many men you killed with them?"

"Too many," Lassiter told him.

"Don't you like being a gunfighter?"

"No, I don't," Lassiter said. "But I don't have a choice anymore."

"What do you mean you don't have a choice?" the boy asked.

"I mean, I can't go anywhere any longer without someone wanting to gun me down," Lassiter replied.

"People wouldn't shoot you if you weren't wearing those guns," the boy suggested. "Why don't you just quit wearing them if you don't like it?"

"I told you, I can't," Lassiter said. It seemed a simple thing to this boy to just put your guns down and hope for the best. "I can't just take off my guns."

"That ain't so," the boy told him. "If you want to, you can just take those guns off and never wear them again."

"Let's go," Stanford said impatiently. "We've got to get out of here."

"Just a minute," Lassiter said before he mounted. He turned to the boy. "I want to believe you're right, son," he said. "But maybe I haven't the courage to take it upon myself to do what you said. Maybe I don't believe I *can* take off these guns and start my life over."

"I wish you would," the boy said. "You're too nice of a man to be killing people all the time."

Lassiter stared at the boy. Stanford finally broke the silence by again urging Lassiter up onto his horse.

"What we hanging around here for, Lassiter?" he growled. "You want us to get caught?"

Lassiter got into one of his saddlebags and dug. Then he leaned over and gave the boy three silver dollars.

"These are for you and nobody else," Lassiter told the boy. "You keep them. Don't give them to your pa or your uncle."

The boy stared at the coins. "It don't cost this much to board your horse," he said. "You gave me way too much."

"That's for taking care of my horse so well," Lassiter told him. "And for being who you are."

The boy stared up at him. "What do you mean?"

"Some day you'll understand," Lassiter said.

Suddenly the form of a man appeared at the other end of the stables.

"Chelsie!" the man yelled. "Who is that with you? Get back away from them."

"Pa!" the boy yelled.

The man turned and ran back toward the church, yelling and shouting that Lassiter and Stanford had escaped from jail. The boy turned and looked up at Lassiter.

"I didn't know he was coming," the boy said apologetically. "I guess I took too long and he came to check on me."

"Don't blame yourself," Lassiter told him. "Maybe I'll see you again someday."

Lassiter kicked his black stallion into a run, and with Jack Stanford close behind, rode out into the morning. The boy stood at the entrance to the livery stable and just stared out. Then he began to run toward the church.

Both Lassiter and Stanford were aware of the yelling

and the men pouring out of the church and into the streets, running for their horses. But they rode hard out from Cheyenne and toward the hills beyond town, putting distance between themselves and the posse that was sure to form. They were safe—at least for the time being.

11

IT WAS HARDY MALONE who was most concerned about Lassiter's breakout. He had been at the front of the church when the livery man, Duke Burns, burst into the funeral service. Burns had announced that Lassiter and Stanford were taking their horses from the stables and that his son, Chelsie, was in grave danger.

To the great annoyance of Clara McCord and her father, Malone had burst from his seat, shouting, "We have to stop them! We have to stop them!" He pushed past the mourners to get out of the church and into the street as fast as he could, raising more than a few eyebrows.

The turmoil in the church overshadowed the service, and many of the men left to join in the chase after Lassiter and Jack Stanford. Trace McCord was torn between joining them and remaining at his daughter's side during her period of grief.

At length he could see there was no real decision; he remained with his daughter.

"They'll catch them without me," McCord told Clara. "We'll bury Allen and worry about everything else later."

Clara looked at her father. "I hope they don't catch them," she said. "Neither of those two have done anything to anyone in this valley. I know that now. I want to prove that Hardy Malone did it."

McCord nodded. "It could be that you're right. It could very well be."

"Then stop Malone and the others from going after them," she said.

"They had no right to break jail," McCord said firmly. "Who's to know if they killed Frank Lund or not."

Clara turned back to the service and remained quiet. The minister finished the service for the mourners who remained in attendance. For Clara, it was hard to concentrate. Her mind was turning over with anger at Hardy Malone. She was convinced that anyone who felt sure about their own innocence would never have acted as he just had.

At the end of the service the crowd passed by the wooden box that held the body of Allen Hutton on their way out of the church and paid their respects. Clara stood at the coffin a moment and let the tears roll down her cheeks, then started for the door.

Clara walked out into the morning on her father's arm, her black veil shielding her eyes from the sunlight. She felt like removing the veil, for something told her that Allen would rest much better now that Lassiter was out of jail.

She allowed her father to help her into the black coach that would take them to the cemetery above town. She felt light on her feet, relieved that there was no one in Frank Lund's jail right now and that Hardy Malone would now be absent from the graveside service.

Trace McCord sensed the ease with which his daughter moved, and commented, "Why do you seem happy all of a sudden?"

"I don't know that I'm happy," she replied. "But I feel a lot better. I feel a lot better for Allen."

McCord nodded at his daughter's statement, not exactly understanding it, but finding no words in response. He sat beside her in silence while she lifted her veil and looked over the landscape, occasionally glancing in the direction where Lassiter and Jack Stanford had lost themselves in the hills and ravines west of town.

"I've made another decision," she suddenly announced. "I intend to ride the red stallion in the Fourth of July horse race."'

"You can't be serious, Clara," Trace McCord said. "That's a grueling race for even the most seasoned of riders."

"I can ride that horse every bit as well as Allen ever could," Clara said quickly. "And that horse won't allow anyone else on his back but me."

"I don't want you to do it, Clara," McCord said. "It's far too dangerous."

"Not on that horse," Clara said. "He's the best horse around here, with the possible exception of Lassiter's black stallion. I know I can win that race. And I intend to."

"I don't want to argue with you, Clara," McCord said. "We'll discuss it later."

As the procession wound its way up to the cemetery, Trace McCord continued to watch his daughter.

She had some determination about her now. She seemed to be over the sense of loss she had awakened with and had taken to the funeral. Now she was different.

Clara didn't wait to have her father ask her to put her veil back down as they neared the spot where Allen Hutton was to be buried. She lowered it, and with her arm linked in his, walked slowly to the grave site.

As she listened to the minister's words about ashes to ashes and dust to dust, she allowed her mind to drift out into the countryside, wondering where Lassiter and Jack Stanford had hidden themselves. Likely they wouldn't be able to stay in one place very long. She knew there wasn't much country that the men of the valley didn't know. Sooner or later they would be found.

They would be found, that is, unless she took a hand in hiding them. She knew the location of a number of Box Y line cabins in the Medicine Bow range a good distance from town. No one would find them there. It would give them a chance to stay out of a hangman's noose long enough for evidence against Hardy Malone to show itself.

As the service over Allen Hutton concluded, Clara found herself determined to find where Lassiter and Jack Stanford might be hiding, so that she could help them. She didn't know how or when she would be able to get away to ride out into the hills, and she knew her father certainly wouldn't let her go alone. But she would find a way.

If there was one thing Clara McCord was determined to do, it was to bring Hardy Malone to justice.

*   *   *

Hardy Malone led the posse through the hills to the west. It was the only place Lassiter and Stanford could have gone to get into rough country fast enough to elude followers. Malone was intent on finding them. He didn't want to stop until Lassiter and Jack Stanford were dead.

There were mixed feelings among the others in the group. Some thought it had been a bad decision to leave Frank Lund bound and gagged in the cell. He was in bad shape from a head wound, and there were those who thought his life was in danger.

It was true that they couldn't find the keys and every second lost was a second gained by Lassiter and Stanford. but there must have been some way of getting to Lund.

Malone didn't care about anything or anybody—only catching up with Lassiter. So they had left with the blacksmith working to cut through the bars and get into the cell.

A number in the posse were wondering why Malone was so obsessed. It was as if he felt personally responsible for seeing to it that the stranger and Jack Stanford were brought to his own brand of justice.

There was one man riding with the posse who was just as determined to see to it that Malone didn't get his obsession fulfilled. Johnny Ridge was going to find out what had happened to Curly, if it was the last thing he did. He wasn't afraid of Malone anymore. He knew Malone couldn't make even one false move now—not with Lassiter free. Everyone was watching Malone carefully, wondering what was driving him so strongly and what he was going to do next. That made things just right for Johnny.

While they stopped in a draw to water their horses and discuss where Lassiter and Stanford might have gone, Johnny noticed something that Malone had, something that had belonged to Curly.

Malone took a gold watch out of his pocket and checked the time. He commented about how long it was taking to get back into the hills.

Johnny controlled his anger as he asked, "Do you always tell time with a dead man's watch?"

Startled, Malone put the watch away quickly.

"What kind of strange question was that?" he asked.

"You know very well," Johnny said. "That watch belonged to Curly. So why have you got it?"

"It's been in my family for years," Malone said gruffly. "It's got my grandfather's initials on it."

"What's this all about?" one of the other hands asked.

"Curly's gone, and he was a good friend of mine," Johnny replied. "Malone was with him just before he disappeared, and I'm trying to get some answers."

Malone turned back to Johnny. He had wanted to avoid any contact with him, but everyone was listening now.

"He told me he wanted to move on," Malone finally said. "He must have drifted out of the valley."

"He didn't say goodbye to anybody," Johnny pointed out. "Doesn't that seem strange?"

"No, it doesn't," Malone said. "He just wanted to get going, he said. Don't ask me why he was in such a hurry."

"You're sure Curly just moved on?" Johnny asked again. "And you're sure that watch isn't his?"

"I told you yes, he just moved on," Malone said, obviously getting angrier.

"Then why didn't you tell anybody that he left?"

Johnny pushed. "You didn't tell anybody until just now, did you?"

Malone shrugged. "I think I told a few hands."

"Which ones?" Johnny pressed.

"Dammit! We haven't got time for this." Malone was fuming. He turned his horse out of the stream and started up the bank.

"Wait a minute, Malone," one of the other men in the posse said. "You're not answering Johnny's questions all that good. I'd like to hear about this visit you had with Curly."

"I said we ain't got time for this," Malone blared, turning his horse. "Are you all coming with me, or not?"

"Who said you're in charge?" the man wanted to know.

"Do *you* want to be in charge?" Malone challenged him. "If you do, take over now. Otherwise, shut up!"

Everyone was startled by Malone's brashness. Everyone except Johnny Ridge. Malone was good at intimidating people, and Johnny knew it. But Johnny wasn't going to slack off Malone one bit.

"You go ahead and lead us after that gunfighter," Johnny spoke up. "That's a good way to hide what you've been up to."

"Maybe we had better have this out here and now," Malone suggested.

"Maybe we had," Johnny agreed.

He quickly drew his gun and trained it on Malone before Malone could pull his own gun. Malone acted as shocked as everyone else.

"Put that gun away, Johnny," one of the other men said. "There'll be no killing here."

"You bet there won't," Johnny agreed. "I don't aim to let him get the drop on me."

"I don't know what's between you two," another one of the posse said, "but it's slowing us down. You two can settle this after we get Jack Stanford and that gunfighter."

Johnny looked around the group. He could see that everyone else agreed with what had been said. No one seemed interested now in getting to the truth about Curly, not even the hand who had spoken up first. It didn't matter what the truth was—that Hardy Malone had killed him. All that mattered was chasing two men who had been pushed into a jail without a real lick of solid evidence against either of them.

Johnny holstered his pistol and glared at the group. Just because nobody knew Curly that well, they were all willing to take Malone's word that he had just drifted off somewhere. Curly hadn't fit in with anyone else, so nobody missed him.

"Maybe you had better ride back to town," one of the posse members suggested to Johnny. "We don't need any more trouble here. We've got enough with Jack Stanford and that gunfighter. You don't need to make it worse."

Johnny noted the hard smile that crossed Malone's face as the other members of the posse agreed. They were bent on one thing, and Malone seemed to carry enough weight among them to override any other sense of right or wrong.

"I'll go, if that's what you all want," Johnny said, turning his horse. "But when this is all over, you can bet that each of you will see that I'm right about Malone."

Malone ignored Johnny and began leading the men once again in the chase for Lassiter and Stanford.

Johnny kicked his horse into a gallop in the other direction and crossed the stream again. He fought the intense rage that was building within him, an anger that almost made him turn around and ride back toward the posse.

He wanted to confront Malone again in the worst way. He wanted to make the posse listen to him. But he knew that wouldn't work and it could cause his own death. If he charged at Malone—especially after the conversation that had just concluded—no one would fault Malone for shooting him.

So Johnny controlled his anger. As soon as he was a ways from the posse, he reined his horse and watched Malone lead the posse deeper into the hills, following what they believed to be the trial left by Lassiter and Stanford. He watched for a time, then smiled.

They could follow that trail all they wanted. He was certain they would never catch up to Lassiter and Stanford. The gunfighter dressed in black was way too smart. He had to be. No doubt this had happened to Lassiter any number of times before—a posse chasing him—and he had eluded them as well.

Johnny spurred his horse and headed back toward town. He decided he would learn the details of the jailbreak and what had happened to Frank Lund. Whatever had happened to Lund, he thought, wasn't enough.

He also wanted to talk to Clara McCord, to see if she thought Malone was guilty. If she did, maybe they could work together in bringing Malone to the justice he deserved.

12

THE DAY WAS GONE and twilight ebbed out its last moments of color through a pale crimson band across the horizon. Lassiter and Stanford sat their horses still, hidden within a patch of pines at the brow of a hill. The posse was less than two hundred yards away, sitting and talking among themselves.

The two men didn't move or speak. If the posse saw them, they would have to shoot it out. Their horses were worn out; the heat of the day had exhausted them. And Jack Stanford was near collapsing from his wound. There would be no more running. Lassiter was just angry enough to put an end to this whole thing, one way or another.

He watched to see what the posse would do, hoping his friend could hold on for just a little while longer. Jack Stanford was stronger than most any other man, but the beating he had taken from Frank Lund would have killed most men and Stanford's pain had finally caught up with him. He had been growing steadily weaker since noon, and they had stopped a number of times for Lassiter to retighten the support around Stanford's chest. The hard riding was hammering his ribs and slamming the blood through his injured head.

Lassiter had feared more than once that his friend would collapse in the saddle. But Stanford was angry enough about the circumstances to keep himself upright. Throughout the whole day he had fought the pain of his head and rib wounds, certain that his final reward would come with the falling sun.

Just a few moments more would spell that relief— either that, or a shootout with the posse.

Finally, a few of the posse mounted and turned their horses as Hardy Malone yelled for them to come back, that they could likely catch up with Lassiter and Stanford in the darkness. But nobody wanted to pursue the two at night but Malone.

Soon the rest of the posse had mounted and turned back for town as well. They had no idea the two men they had been chasing were nearby, in the shadows, and at the end of their ability to run.

Lassiter watched as Malone remained behind. Malone held his nervous horse and studied the shadows along the hillside. It seemed he wanted to make one last effort.

Lassiter rested his hand on his rifle scabbard, seriously considering dropping Hardy Malone from his horse. Then Malone turned and joined the others. Lassiter eased his grip on the rifle.

The posse had come well within rifle range more than once, and Lassiter had been sorely tempted to end Malone's life then. But each time he had thought better of it. Killing Malone would leave him even more open to accusation in the death of Allen Hutton.

The posse was finally gone, and the red streaks of

twilight filtered out to black. Lassiter and Stanford dismounted.

"I can't take another day of this," Stanford announced. "If they come back out after us, I say we make a stand."

"They'll be back out after us," Lassiter promised. "But we don't stand a chance against so many."

Stanford was sitting with his back and head resting against a tree. Only his tortured face was partially lit in the waning light.

"We don't stand a chance if we have to ride like this again," he said. "Why don't you just go on? I can't make it any farther."

"I'm not going anywhere without you," Lassiter said firmly.

Stanford tried to smile. "You never did have much sense, did you?"

"We'll get out of this," Lassiter said. "We just need a plan."

"If we don't find a place to hide out, we're done," Stanford said. "I tell you, I'll die before I go back to that jail and put up with Frank Lund anymore."

Lassiter thought for a time, while Stanford grimaced in the shadows. Lassiter knew he should take Stanford to a doctor; but there was little chance of that. All he could hope for was some relief from the chase.

After more thinking, Lassiter concluded that the only chance they had was to obtain help from somebody who was on their side. Johnny Ridge was the first person who came to mind, but there wasn't any way of knowing where he was or how much help he could be.

The only other choice they had was to appeal to Clara McCord. It seemed like a long shot, but Lassiter brought it up to Stanford anyway.

Stanford tried to laugh through the pain. "Maybe you'd just as soon be hung at the Box Y as in town. That it?"

"What's your suggestion?" Lassiter asked him. "We know they're coming back out after us. And if we just run, we'll find Wanted posters waiting for us in every town we come to. We'd just as well get this whole thing ironed out now."

"Do what you think is best," Stanford managed. "I don't feel up to making any decisions right now. I just need some sleep."

Lassiter thought some more and concluded he would go to the Box Y and let Stanford rest. That way he could find Clara and talk to her without worrying about having to flee with Stanford if something went wrong.

There was only one real concern Lassiter had about getting to Clara. Hardy Malone would most likely take the posse there, if for nothing more than to check in with McCord and show that he was doing his community duty. And possibly to try and recruit more men for the following day.

If that was the case, it would be hard to get to talk to Clara without a confrontation with Malone. But there was little choice to do anything else but ride to the Box Y.

Lassiter helped Stanford unsaddle and then picketed his horse for the night. He spread a blanket over his friend and put his guns close.

"I'm going to take off now," Lassiter told him. "I hope to be back before dawn."

"Aren't you going to tell me a bedtime story?" Stanford asked jokingly.

"Maybe when I get back," Lassiter said.

He left his friend fighting the pain to fall asleep, and

got onto his black stallion. The clouds parted to show a nearly full moon, and Lassiter took one last look to where the posse had disappeared. Then he started for the Box Y.

Clara was on the porch with her father when Hardy Malone led the posse into the yard. She and her father had been expecting him, as word had come that they had given up the chase for the night.

Clara knew Malone was happy with his position as leader of the posse. Frank Lund was bedridden with a concussion, which he said had come from a blow with his own pistol—delivered by Lassiter. Lund wouldn't be much help to anybody for at least the next couple of days.

Malone pulled his horse to a halt ahead of the others in the posse. He was angry with the rest of the men because they hadn't wanted to remain out with him on the chase for Lassiter and Stanford.

"These men have families, Malone," McCord pointed out. "You can't blame them if they don't want to pursue two killers in the dark."

Clara looked sideways at her father. She wondered if he would ever open up his mind enough to know who the killers in this valley really were.

"I'd like to take some of your hands, then, at daylight," Malone said. "I know we can ride them down by tomorrow noon at the latest."

"I'll be going with you, Malone," McCord said. "If you take any of my men, I'll be in charge. Is that understood?"

Malone nodded. "I just want to be sure and get them. Who knows who they'll kill next."

McCord then talked to the entire posse as a whole. "I don't care if you with families want to give this up.

Those who want to stay, take a place in the barn and we'll go back out at dawn.''

Malone was looking at McCord as if he might be invited to spend the night in the house. But McCord caught him looking at Clara and decided to make things clear right away.

"I want everybody to stay in the barn," he said, "and take turns on night watch at the corrals."

The men nodded and turned their horses. Malone reluctantly moved his horse in among them. When they were gone, Clara turned again to her father.

"Why don't you ask Malone about the watch?" she said. "Johnny Ridge must know what he's talking about."

Johnny Ridge had come in earlier, telling that he had seen Malone with Curly's watch and how he was told to leave the posse.

"We'll wait for all that until after we get Jack Stanford and that gunfighter back behind bars," McCord said. "I don't know how much faith to put in Johnny anyway. He's pretty hot about most things he wants to make a point on, and I don't know how clearly he thinks."

"I'm not worried about what he *thinks*," Clara said. "I'm concerned about what he *feels*."

They turned and went back into the house for the evening meal. The housekeeper was waiting for them, and sat down with them. McCord ate hungrily. He wanted to turn in soon, to be rested for the hard ride after Lassiter and Jack Stanford come sunup.

But Clara had a hard time with her meal. She thought more and more about Hardy Malone and became more and more concerned. He was the cause of all of this, she knew, and it wasn't going to be easy convincing her father.

She got up and went outside. Her father followed her, and she told him what her concerns were about Malone.

"I told you, we'll look into it once we get those other two back in jail," he said.

"What if Malone shoots them?" she asked.

"I'll see to it he doesn't. Now, come back inside and finish your meal."

Later on in the evening Clara took a lantern back out to the porch and paced. Each time she thought of Allen Hutton, she wondered what her life would have been like had he not been killed. And every time she thought of him, she thought of Hardy Malone.

Johnny Ridge came back into her mind. "That gold watch was Curly's," she remembered him telling her father earlier. "But no one would believe me. Malone is a killer, and no one wants to notice."

Clara was now hoping she would get a chance to somehow prove that Malone had killed her fiancé. It seemed entirely plausible that Malone had killed Curly to cover up the rumor surrounding Malone's brother and his death at the hands of Allen Hutton. But there was no way to prove that now, either.

"When are you going to bed, Clara?" she heard her father ask from the door.

"Father, I can't sleep," Clara said. "Just go ahead and retire yourself, if you wish to. I'll go along later."

"I don't like you up alone, especially under the circumstances," McCord told his daughter.

"There is no need to worry," Clara assured him. "The entire ranch is well secured. Besides, I don't know why you would think I would be in any danger anyway."

"You can never tell what will happen," McCord said.

"Go to bed, Father," Clara said again. "I'll be along shortly. I just need some time out here to myself."

McCord nodded. "Very well. I'll see you in the morning."

When her father was gone, Clara moved to the edge of the porch and lifted her eyes to the night sky. She had been in this very same place on the porch many times with Allen, looking into the heavens and pointing out stars and planets. It had been a favorite hobby of his—learning the constellations and the movement of the planets. He had even found a book on the subject.

Thinking about it made Clara miss him terribly. Tears formed in her eyes, and they swelled out and down her cheeks. But she concluded that she should get over her mourning and go ahead with her life.

She had just finished rubbing the tears away from her face when she heard a pebble hit the boards of the porch beside her. At first it startled her. Then she realized that someone had thrown it to indicate their presence to her.

It occurred to her that only one man would want to see her and not have anyone else know about it—Lassiter. But she couldn't see him, and she didn't want to make any noise that would rouse her father, or anyone else.

Clara stepped down off the porch and peered into the shadows. She was even more certain now that Lassiter had thrown the pebble. Anyone who meant her harm would not have given her warning.

Finally, she saw the shadow of a man move a ways out from the side of the house into the open. He stayed out of the light of the lantern on the porch. She saw him wave his hand to have her come down to him.

For a moment Clara had misgivings. What if it

wasn't Lassiter? What if it was and he meant to trick her? Using her as a hostage would be a smart move.

She watched him for a time. He seemed patient, as if understanding her fear. He was not a man who was worried about what she might do; he seemed to know that she was on his side.

Finally, Clara regained her composure and moved slowly down into the shadows. She followed him farther away from the house, to a grove of trees a ways back in the yard, and settled down on the ground to talk to him.

"You are our only chance to get Malone off our backs," she heard him say. "Will you help us?"

"I don't know what I can do," she told him.

"Can't you get your father to call off the chase?" he asked. "If he said stop, everyone would do just that."

"Everyone but Hardy Malone," Clara said.

"And that would be good," Lassiter told her. "That way, people would finally begin to wonder."

"I'll do what I can," Clara promised. "But first I've got to hide you out. The place is swarming with men, including Malone."

"Where can we go?" Lassiter asked.

"I'll take you to a cabin, west, in the mountains," Clara said. "You'll be safely hidden there until I can get my father to listen to me."

"You're taking a big chance, and I thank you for it," Lassiter said.

"I want Hardy Malone to pay for what he did just as much as you do," Clara explained.

Lassiter told her where he and Stanford had stopped for the night. She knew the place from the way he described the country.

"Hurry and go now," she told Lassiter. "I'll see you tomorrow."

Clara then heard her father calling for her from the porch. She jumped to her feet, her head turned toward the house. She looked back and Lassiter was gone.

"Clara, where are you?" she heard her father call again.

She hurried back to the porch, where he was waiting, half crazed with worry.

"What in the hell are you doing, Clara?" he asked.

"I just wanted to get some air," she said. "I'm sorry. I didn't mean to concern you."

"Please, come inside now," he said. "I can't take much more of this."

"Very well," Clara said. "I didn't mean to get you so upset."

She walked ahead of her father, up onto the porch and into the house. He brought the lantern in and set it on a table before blowing it out. She could see the strain in his face as he turned to her.

"I wish you wouldn't take so many chances," he said.

"And I wish you wouldn't worry so much about me, Father," she said. "I'm in no danger, I can assure you of that."

She wached him go back to his bedroom, and then retired to her own for the night. She knew he wouldn't understand if she tried to tell him she wanted to help Lassiter and Jack Stanford. He certainly wouldn't allow her to do it.

There was no sense in falling asleep, she finally concluded. She would wait until the first crack of light and go down to the corral. No one would be suspicious of an early morning ride; she had gone with Allen many times to the hills to watch the sun rise.

But she knew she would have to be gone in a hurry, for her father was an early riser. And she knew Hardy Malone and the others would be getting back to the chase early as well. She would just have to beat them all and hope she got away before they discovered she was gone.

13

Dawn was a glint of reddish-pink in the east when Lassiter arrived back to the patch of trees where Jack Stanford rested. His head had cleared considerably from the day before, but he was still suffering considerably from his injuries.

His ribs were as sore as they had ever been, and he wished he could do something more than just wrap them. But he considered himself lucky that none of them were broken, and decided he could live with the pain.

Though he felt better, Stanford's attitude seemed to Lassiter to have taken a turn for the worse.

"I don't know what good getting better is going to do me," he said, as Lassiter took a seat next to him on the ground. "This entire valley wants to put a noose around my neck."

"Don't think that way, Jack," Lassiter told him. "I talked to Clara, and she knows a place we can hide out until this gets straightened out."

"What do you mean?" he asked. "She didn't get her father to call off the posse?"

"That can't be done in just the blink of an eye," Lassiter pointed out. "It's going to take some time to convince him that Hardy Malone bears investigating before we even go to trial."

"So Clara's going to take us to a secret spot?" Stanford asked.

"That's what she said. She's supposed to meet us here before too long."

"That's interesting," Stanford said, shaking his head. "Clara wants to save our hides. You know, she didn't say a word on my behalf when I was accused of stealing her father's horses. Why the sudden change of heart?"

"Maybe she wants to set things straight?" Lassiter suggested. "Don't question it; just go with it."

"Maybe it has more to do with you than it does me," Stanford said. "Maybe she wants to get to know you better."

Lassiter looked at his friend closely. Finally, he smiled. "If I didn't know better, Jack, I'd think you were jealous."

Stanford bristled at the remark, but was forced to hold himself in restraint due to the pain it caused him. He had no intention of letting on that Clara still held a place inside of him that he couldn't release.

Lassiter knew that Jack Stanford could get through just about anything—as long as he wasn't close to dying. What was left between him and Clara to iron out was none of his concern, and he didn't even discuss it with his friend. He didn't want it getting in the way of their unity. Should that happen, there would be a lot of difficulty in staying ahead of whoever might come after them. Infighting was the last thing they needed right now.

Lassiter felt even more concern about circumstances if Clara didn't show up. He fully understood that she wanted to help them and work with them to bring Hardy Malone to justice; there was no question about that. But he was also knew it would be difficult for her to get away from her father and the others without being stopped.

He was certain, though, that there would be some kind of words between his friend and Clara. He could see now how much Stanford still cared for her.

"I didn't mean to hit any sore spots," Lassiter apologized. "Let's just take this a step at a time. We'll hide out and hope for the best on Clara's part. We haven't got much of a choice otherwise."

Stanford nodded. He took a few deep breaths and looked into the dawn sky. The heat would come again and make the chase that much worse. And with Clara coming, there could be other heat to contend with. It would be an interesting day, no question about that.

"Did she say where this hideout was?" Stanford finally asked.

"West, in the mountains, is what she told me," Lassiter answered.

Stanford nodded. "I've got a pretty good idea where it is. I wish we had something to eat."

Lassiter had already begun to chew on a small piece of bark. Its flavor was strong, but he knew the fluids he swallowed would give him strength for the upcoming ride.

"There's bound to be some supplies up there," Lassiter finally said. "But for now we can make due with something to chew on, just to get us through."

He tried to hand his friend a piece of bark, which Stanford pushed away.

"I don't eat trees," Stanford growled. "There's bound to be food up there. I can wait."

Waiting was getting to be hard, though. Stanford acted like he didn't want to go, and then like he did. He was caught in the middle. But it was his life—as well as Lassiter's—that was at stake, and he knew there was no real choice but to follow Clara to the hideout.

Stanford felt pangs of guilt at the circumstances. He had wanted this to be a fun time for Lassiter, a payback to him for saving his life those years past. Now it seemed ironic that he should have his friend come a long way to see him and end up running for his life.

"I'll bet you wish you hadn't come all the way up here for that damned horse race now, don't you?" Stanford asked.

"Don't be so hard on yourself," Lassiter told him. "You had no way of knowing things would turn out like this."

Stanford snorted. "You might have known, though. It seems everytime we get together, we've got our backs to the wall."

"We'll get out of it," Lassiter assured him. "We have before."

"What happens if you don't ride in that race?" Stanford asked. "Is that going to bother you?"

"Has the race started yet?" Lassiter asked.

Stanford looked at Lassiter with a puzzled frown. "You know it hasn't," he said. "It's not the Fourth of July yet."

"Good," Lassiter said with a smile. "Then let's not worry about it until time for the race."

Lassiter and Stanford stretched their legs and watered their horses, looking all around for signs of anyone who might be coming. There was little chance they would miss anyone, as the location among the trees afforded a good view of their backtrail. Anyone approaching would have to come into view miles away.

"This is a lot like the location in Porter Draw," Lassiter commented. "Malone took a spot like this and shot down into the bottom. He couldn't hardly miss."

While the horses drank and snorted themselves to contentment, Lassiter thought more about his first day in the valley. Stanford sensed he was reliving it.

"I can still see Allen Hutton falling from his horse," Lassiter said. "I guess I'll be seeing that for quite a while."

As hardened as Lassiter was to death, he still couldn't get used to watching a man fall from his horse with a bullet in his back. There was something about the expression on a man's face that left the onlooker haunted for a long time to come. The shock and surprise was different when a man faced his opponent and lost. There was something about dying and not even seeing where it had come from that made it worse.

"I can say with certainty that I'm glad I didn't see that," Stanford said. "I didn't like Allen Hutton, but a man shouldn't have to die that way."

The two men mounted up again and took their time riding to where they had camped for the night. Daylight was flashing gold across the land, and the birds were bringing in the new day with enthusiasm. With all the peace, it seemed to Lassiter as if his life should be different now.

It brought his mind to the boy at the livery stable

who had told him he could end all his days of running from his past by merely laying down his guns and walking away from them. That was a possibility, Lassiter thought. But it would be hard to be unarmed and stand in front of a man who wanted to kill you.

Perhaps the trick was in what the boy had said: If you really want to, and have the courage, you can do it. In the right frame of mind, a person could stand unarmed and not worry about his life; Lassiter knew this, for he had seen it happen before.

But he didn't know if he could become someone like that. The twin Colts, with their shiny black handles, had become a part of him—like an extension of his very being. Changing that would take a great deal of time and determination.

Lassiter looked at Stanford and turned his thoughts to what lay before them. They were in a situation that meant life or death, and no amount of wondering about the future could change that. Things in the here and now had to be sorted out right away, or there might be no tomorrow.

All that was left to do now was to hope for Clara's arrival. If she came to help them, it could mean getting out of the mess fairly soon. If she didn't come, it would mean they would have to leave the valley and watch for Wanted posters wherever they went from then on.

Johnny Ridge rode with the posse once again. They were just an hour from the Box Y ranch headquarters, and each man was riding as hard as he could.

This time Johnny knew he wouldn't be told to leave, for Trace McCord had personally asked him to go. "I want to get this thing between you and Malone straightened out," Johnny remembered McCord saying. That was something Johnny was looking forward to.

But Johnny knew Trace McCord's mind wasn't on anyone but his daughter at the present time. She had left on the red stallion very early, just early enough to get a good head start. But she had been spotted by Hardy Malone, and he had rushed to the ranch house to tell McCord.

Now all was general havoc, as McCord was nearly delirious with worry over his daughter's absence. Malone had watched her ride west, and he knew she was headed for the place where they had abandoned the chase the day before. He was now kicking himself for not having continued the pursuit into the darkness.

There was talk and wonderment now about what Clara's motives were. Johnny didn't want to ask McCord why he thought his daughter had acted as she had. It was obvious she didn't want either Lassiter or Jack Stanford to hang. Some wondered which man she was most worried about.

Most of the speculation was about Stanford, for everyone knew Clara had been friendly with him before Allen Hutton's arrival in the valley. They had spent considerable time together, and it was common knowledge that Stanford had never gotten over her leaving him for Allen Hutton. It seemed reasonable to conclude that Stanford could have hired Lassiter to kill Hutton.

But now that Clara had taken off to help them, there were doubts raised as to whether either of the two men had anything to do with Hutton's death. Surely, everyone figured, she wouldn't be helping them if she didn't believe they were innocent.

All Johnny could think of now was the courage Clara had shown in taking off on her own and doing what she thought was best. Whether or not everyone thought Lassiter and Stanford were guilty, no one could fault Clara for making up her own mind.

Johnny knew Trace McCord was worried about the impression this whole thing was giving everyone. It made them think that possibly she was still attached to Stanford in some way, though Johnny knew that wasn't the sole reason she had taken off in behalf of the two men. That she felt they were innocent had to be more important to her, and that there was some other man who might be responsible for her fiancé's death.

Johnny knew his constant confrontations with Malone had set people to wondering as well. Whether or not that had done a lot of good was a matter of question. But there was certainty now in the fact that Trace McCord wanted him as a member of the posse, and wanted to learn more about Hardy Malone.

Lassiter and Stanford had just gotten settled in the trees again when Lassiter noticed a rider approaching from the direction of the Box Y. The rider was still two to three miles away, but the billowing column of dust showed that the horse was going fast.

"It looks like she's finally made it," Lassiter commented. "I was beginning to wonder, there, for a time."

Stanford rose to his feet beside Lassiter. "I'd bet her father and the others aren't far behind her," he speculated.

Lassiter agreed. He knew that Clara would want to get to them as soon as she could, but she certainly wouldn't want to wear down her horse riding hard to find them. The only explanation was that she had not gotten a good enough head start.

Lassiter knew soon enough that the rider on the red stallion was indeed Clara. She was certainly in a hurry, which meant trouble. Not many miles behind was the dust of a large group of riders. The posse hadn't taken long at all to get reassembled and on the trail.

Lassiter and Stanford mounted and met Clara at the edge of the trees. As she pulled her horse to a stop, Lassiter noticed the quick, hard looks that took place between her and Stanford. But there was no time to discuss the past; Clara was troubled about something other than Jack Stanford.

"What happened?" Lassiter asked. "Did someone stop you before you could leave?"

"No," she said, out of breath. "But somebody saw me, I just know it."

"You didn't see who watched you leave?" Lassiter asked. "Are you sure anyone did?"

Clara turned and pointed into the distance. The large plume of dust on the horizon was growing.

"I know they're after me," she said. "I knew my father would notice I was gone. But someone else must have seen me, otherwise they wouldn't be so close behind."

"They're riding that hard because of your father," Stanford said. "I know that man pretty well. And he won't give up until he's caught up with us."

Clara looked hard again at Stanford. "You just let me take care of this," she said. "They won't catch up. You know that."

"Lead on," Lassiter said to her. "We haven't got time for arguments."

Lassiter and Stanford followed Clara deep into the foothills that rolled to the west. It would be a faster run, Lassiter knew, than the previous day, which was already evident in the way Clara led them out at a strong pace. It would not be a circle game, as it had been the day before, but an all-out chase—a game to get rid of Malone and the posse, so there would be no way the posse could know where they were headed. And it would test everyone to the limit.

14

As THEY RODE INTO the upper foothills and then into the mountains, Lassiter realized they could not keep up a pace this fast. The altitude and the steep terrain were wearing down the horses. They were going to have to rely on trail tricks to throw the posse off.

Clara proved to be a very smart leader. There were places where she told Lassiter and Stanford to break off from her and go up different draws. They would later meet at some distant ridge, and the splitting up of tracks would slow the posse by forcing it into decisions on how to follow the diverging trails.

As the morning moved into midday, the heat rose again and the air grew hot. The only relief was under the trees, and the higher they climbed, the more the trees gave shade. It kept the horses in much better shape than riding in the open, as they had the previous day, but the strain of the climb was going to wear them down before long.

They moved at a good pace throughout the day, but

still did not outdistance the group of riders behind them. At a high stream they stopped to rest and water the horses. Lassiter finally asked Clara why the posse was staying so close.

"Does your father have any idea which line cabin you're taking us to?" he asked.

Clara talked over the horses' heavy panting. "It would seem that way. But I've decided to let them think that and take you to a different one. We'll travel down this creek a ways and then come out in the rocks above where the cabin sits."

Again Lassiter was amazed at the techniques Clara was using to shake a group of followers. Traveling down a creek to let the running water hide your tracks was an old trick, but not one usually used by a lady used to good living.

"Tell me, where did you learn all these trail tricks?" Lassiter asked.

Clara smiled. She turned to Stanford. "Why don't you tell him, Jack?" she said.

Stanford blushed. "Clara was with me a couple of times when I was out looking over my cattle. We knew each other well enough then that I could show her some of our old-time tricks when we were out on the trail."

Lassiter nodded. These two, he concluded, had shared a lot of experiences together. They had obviously been a lot closer than most people had suspected. It made him wonder what had caused Clara to fall for Allen Hutton the way she had.

"That was fun while it lasted, Jack," Clara said. She tried to make her voice sound as if the statement were final. But both men heard in her tone that she wasn't sure what was final anymore.

They rode in silence. Lassiter followed Clara upstream, with Stanford riding behind. He knew they were riding to save themselves and to keep their hopes alive of being cleared of Allen Hutton's death. That was foremost, and that would be the hardest.

But Lassiter knew also that both Stanford and Clara were riding back into the past—where they had once been so close. All of this was going to complicate things to a great degree. And he hoped it didn't end up causing them all a great deal of trouble.

They rode in silence the rest of the way to the point among the rocks where they left the stream. After crossing a low, wooded ridge, Lassiter spotted a small cabin nestled in the timber along another creek that flowed just below. Unless you knew just exactly how to find the cabin, there was no way you could see it from anywhere but the ridge.

"I think my father has been over most of this country out here," Clara said. "But I'm sure he doesn't know about this cabin. We've never had any of our cattle roam this high up."

Lassiter looked at Stanford. It was obvious he had known about the cabin before. And it was equally as obvious to Lassiter that he had been here with Clara.

The inside of the cabin showed it received little use. Most of the line cabins, as Clara had pointed out, were at a lower elevation. They were used most in the fall and winter months, and cattle never roamed this high up past September. By Thanksgiving the snow was usually too deep to even get to the cabin.

Lassiter and Stanford hobbled their horses nearby and brought their saddles in. It was much cooler up high, and they were all grateful for the relief. The rest was much needed, but Clara appeared anxious to be on her way. She didn't say much, but paced around the cabin and then outside, talking about saddling her horse again to get ready to leave.

Lassiter concluded it was her feelings from being here with Jack Stanford that had made her uneasy now.

"Don't be in such a rush," he said. "You haven't even had time to hardly catch your breath."

"I haven't got time for that," she said. "I've got to get back down to the ranch."

Lassiter nodded. Stanford acted as if he wasn't paying any attention.

"When I finally get my father convinced that you're innocent," she continued, "I'll come back up for you. There won't be anyone who will find you here."

"How do you intend to get back down out of here without someone seeing you, Clara?" Stanford asked. It was the first thing he had said to her since their discussion about trail tricks in the creek below.

"You know how I'll get out, Jack," she said. "The same way we got in. That's the only way, unless I go down and clear around. Then it would take another full day to get back to the ranch. My father would die of worry in the meantime."

"Everyone's going to be watching," Stanford said. "Why don't you just wait until it's dark and then go back out?"

Clara took a deep breath. "Jack, I can't do that. I have to get back." She turned for the door.

"We're both much obliged to you for bringing us up here," Lassiter said, speaking for both himself and Stanford. "Be careful on the way back out."

"I'll see you again before long," Clara promised.

She remounted the red stallion and made her way back up to the ridge from the cabin. Lassiter watched from the door, while Stanford looked out a window in the opposite direction.

"Why didn't you tell me that you and Clara were once that close?" Lassiter asked.

"Because it's none of your damn business," Stanford said flatly.

"Maybe not, but it sure would have made it easier to understand some things," Lassiter said. "Now I can see why everyone is so sure you brought me here to kill Allen Hutton, and why Malone thinks he's got things his way."

Stanford turned from the window. "Are you saying if you'd have known all this, you wouldn't have come up here to ride in the race for me?"

"No, of course not," Lassiter said. "But I could have at least learned a few more things from Clara when she came to talk to me in the jail the other night. She didn't tell me a thing."

"She didn't know you," Stanford said in her defense. "Why would you expect her to tell you her life story?"

"Have it your way, Jack," Lassiter said, and turned back to the window,

Stanford slammed his fist against the long wall in frustration. He knew Lassiter had come blindly into a situation that could have cost him his life, and still could. And he didn't want to appear cold to his friend.

"Look, I'm sorry about all this, Lassiter," he finally said. "I had no idea Malone was gunning for Hutton. No idea."

"You couldn't have known," Lassiter agreed. "There was no way anyone could have predicted what happened. No one even knows Malone that well, and there wasn't any reason anyone would have thought Allen Hutton was going to be shot."

"There's still the situation between Clara and me," Stanford said. "I guess I wanted to win that race in the worst way. And to have you in it with your black stallion would have given me way better than even odds that I could have made Allen Hutton look bad. Maybe I thought that would make a difference to Clara, I don't know. I wish now I'd never sent for you."

"What's done is done," Lassiter told Stanford. "Stop worrying about it. Just try and get your feelings about Clara sorted out. Maybe you two can still get back together."

Stanford looked quickly to Lassiter. "I don't want that," he said.

"Are you sure?"

"I'm sure."

Lassiter shrugged. "That's up to you. For now, let's just keep our fingers crossed that Clara gets out of here without the posse seeing her."

The posse was stopped and there was a tension in the air, a strong tension. As the men watered their horses at the stream, Johnny watched Hardy Malone closely. Malone was smiling broadly to himself.

Things had changed a great deal; Trace McCord was going back to the ranch. His horse had thrown a shoe. It was getting late in the afternoon, and they had lost the trail here at the creek. Now all the men were discussing what they would do—either go on or return to the ranch with McCord.

McCord was certain about one thing: he wasn't going to give up, no matter what. But if he continued to ride, he would be taking the chance of laming his horse severely. And with as much riding as was left to catch up to Clara, his horse wouldn't be able to hold up.

"Maybe we should all go back and start over in the morning," Johnny suggested.

"No," Malone said quickly. "We'll lose too much time. Besides, we might spot them moving around up here. We can't all go back."

There was discussion about how the posse should continue. Some of the men were thinking of giving up anyway, since they had entered the upcoming horse race. It was set to begin in just two days.

"I'll pay anyone who stays with this posse a hundred dollars, no matter what the outcome," McCord finally said. "I want to find my daughter and return her safely to the ranch."

Some of the men took McCord up on the offer, while others decided they were going to chance winning bigger money in the race. McCord cared little about the race anymore. But he had to go back and get a fresh mount to keep up the chase for Clara. And he was emphatic about being along when they started again.

"I want you all to camp here," McCord told the posse. "I intend to bring Frank Lund back with me first thing in the morning."

"There's still some daylight left," Malone argued. "We can go on without you."

"I don't want that," McCord said firmly. He was looking directly at Malone as he added, "Wait until I get back with Lund before you move ahead. I don't want to take any chances with my daughter's life. I want to be there when we find them. Do you understand?"

Malone nodded, his head down. Two of the Box Y hands went back with McCord for more horses while the remaining body of the posse remained behind. Malone was fretting while he and some of the men collected firewood. Some of the men went into the trees and found timber grouse that were common up here—fool hens, they called them.

There was still a good hour until nightfall, and Malone continued to fret. The other men worked to get a couple of fires going, and soon they were cooking grouse over an open fire and talking about the plans for the next day.

By now everyone had concluded that Clara was helping Lassiter and Stanford. McCord had, too, though he hadn't said as much. A good many of the men knew any number of line cabins up in the area. But all of them could be seen from a good distance, and they knew Clara would have found a better place for the fugitives.

Malone talked once about going out on his own to find them. A number of the men spoke up and told him he had better stay in camp. Going against Trace McCord wasn't good for anybody.

Johnny was getting angrier. He knew Malone was up to doing anything to clear himself of Allen Hutton's killing. And getting Lassiter and Stanford would just about do it. He couldn't allow that to happen.

Though he knew he was risking hs own life by being anywhere near Malone, Johnny didn't intend to let Malone out of his sight. His friend Curly was uppermost on his mind. Losing Curly was going to be hard to get over, and Johnny didn't intend to let Malone get a moment's peace until everyone knew what was really going on.

One of the men, standing a ways off from the fires, pointed out a lone rider coming toward camp. The men ran to their horses, ready to mount up. But the rider turned out to be a boy—the stablehand, Chelsie Burns.

Johnny knew Chelsie from a time when the boy brought some freshly shod horses out to the Box Y. He could see that Chelsie had been riding hard. Johnny held his horse while he got down.

"I came out to find Mr. McCord," the boy said. "His hired hands came into town, and my pa sent me out here."

Johnny told him that McCord had gone back to the ranch with a lame horse.

"It's important I find him," the boy said. "Some of his hands were moving cows this morning up in the hills behind the ranch and found a dead man."

Johnny immediately looked at Malone, whose face turned an ashen white.

"Who was the dead man?" Johnny asked Chelsie, his eyes still on Malone.

"A hand who worked there, is what they said," the boy answered. "I think his name was Curly."

Now everyone looked hard at Malone. Without hesitating an instant, Malone pulled his gun and shot Johnny. Luckily, Johnny was moving to get out of the way, so the bullet missed his chest. It struck him high in the left shoulder instead, spinning him around and to the ground.

Malone then promised the same to anyone else who tried to make a move on him. Though they outnumbered him, no one wanted to be killed. Everyone watched while Malone backed to his horse, mounted, then kicked the animal into a dead run for the timber.

Chelsie ran to Johnny, who was coming to his knees, holding his shoulder. He was lucky; though the bullet had chipped the top of the collarbone, it had done little other damage. Johnny's shoulder would be sore for a good long time, but he was in no danger of dying.

Some of the men had run to their horses and were now giving chase after Malone. The sun had fallen, but there was some sparse light left in the western sky. As much as Johnny wanted to see Malone behind bars, he knew that the men shouldn't be going after him just now.

Johnny got to his feet and leaned against Chelsie as he watched the others mount and ride blindly after Malone. Intent on catching him, they weren't in the least bit cautious. Johnny could see that Malone had come out of the timber and was now silhouetted against the sky at the top of the hill. He was pulling his rifle from its scabbard.

Though Malone was shooting offhanded from the back of his horse, he managed to hit one man and put down three horses. One man jumped clear of his horse, but two others looked as if they sustained serious injuries when their wounded horses fell with them.

Malone laughed as he turned his horse and disappeared into the shadows.

Some of the men took wild shots at him as he rode over the hill. There was a lot of confusion now as the others scrambled for cover, some getting ready to shoot into the darkness. No one was sure of where Malone had gone or if he intended to come back and shoot again.

Johnny sat with Chelsie in the cover of the trees and waited. Chelsie held his breath for a time, then relaxed when everyone started to come out and gather around camp again. Malone was gone now, and there wasn't anyone who was going after him.

"I guess it's men like Malone who make men like

Mr. Lassiter have to wear guns all the time," Chelsie commented offhandedly.

"I think you're right," Johnny told him. "I think that's absolutely right."

"Do you think Malone will be back?" Chelsie asked.

"It's hard to say, but I don't think so," Johnny answered. There were already some men helping bandage his shoulder. "He's done enough damage for one day. But I'm sure he'll be ready again once the sun rises."

15

THE ONE MAN THAT Malone had managed to shoot was found dead—one of the Box Y hands. Another one to add to the count, along with Curly, Johnny thought bitterly. Trace McCord was losing men to Malone faster than he could hire them. There had to be an end put to it soon.

Johnny's shoulder was beginning to stiffen up. He watched with Chelsie while the others helped to get the two wounded men back down into camp. Both of them had knees that were badly sprained from falling with their horses.

Despite the pain, Johnny had his rifle ready at all times. While some of the men attended to the wounded or patrolled the edge of camp, Johnny sat with Chelsie and drank coffee. Everyone was now in a sullen mood, and Chelsie was uncomfortable.

"Don't worry about Malone coming back," Johnny tried to assure him. "He'd be foolish to do that."

"Maybe," Chelsie said, not entirely convinced, "but I sure wish Mr. Lassiter was here."

"He would be a big help right now," Johnny agreed. "If only he knew he didn't have to run anymore."

"Do you know Mr. Lassiter very well?" Chelsie asked.

"I've talked to him a few times," Johnny replied. "I know he didn't kill Allen Hutton. But I guess we all know that now, don't we?"

"I talked to him when he broke jail," Chelsie went on. "He's a nice man. But why is he a gunfighter?"

Johnny shrugged. "Sometimes a man finds himself on the run for something he didn't do or for defending himself when others don't see it that way. Any number of things can happen. Then a man is branded and he can't get out of it."

Chelsie nodded. "I suppose so. I'm afraid that I don't think it's fair."

"It's not," Johnny agreed. "But when the cards are dealt, you have to play them."

This time Chelsie didn't nod. "I think that people can deal their own cards. I don't think they have to have things happen to them all the time. If I can, I want to go to school and learn how to talk to people about how they can help themselves and not be unhappy. I want to be that kind of doctor."

Johnny turned and stared at Chelsie. He had heard of such doctors, in bigger places like Denver, who could help you with your thinking. But most people out here had no idea about that kind of thing, let alone a young boy who worked in a livery stable.

"What made you think about that, Chelsie?" Johnny finally asked.

"I talked to one of those kind of men one time," Chelsie said. "He told a woman who had lost her baby from the coughs that her life was just beginning. She was only sixteen. He showed her how to sit quietly and talk to God every day about her baby. And it helped her. He saw me watching him and we talked later."

"What did he tell you?" Johnny asked.

"He told me this country out here needs more people who can doctor people's feelings in their heads, and not just their bodies. He said they work together— the body and the mind—and the spirit, too, he said. I believe him. I want to learn how to do that."

"Maybe you will some day, Chelsie," Johnny assured him. "I think you can do just about anything you want."

Chelsie went over to lay down and relax. It was hard for him; Johnny could see that he wouldn't get much sleep. He wondered how they could ever find Lassiter and Jack Stanford now, especially with Clara hiding them out. And with Malone up there, they would have to ride a whole lot slower.

Johnny tried to make himself relax as best he could. He had nothing for the pain, and his shoulder was stiffening up even more. It made him that much angrier at Hardy Malone, and he vowed he would stay with the posse until they caught Malone. That was one man he wouldn't allow to get away.

Clara had been gone less than an hour when Lassiter and Stanford heard the shooting. There were a number of shots that brought them up from a resting position and out the door of the cabin.

It sounded like it was a good distance away—possibly somewhere near the place they had begun their ride down the creek. Neither Lassiter nor Stanford thought Clara would have taken the same way back, but they were still very concerned.

They ran to where their horses were picketed, grazing in a nearby meadow, and saddled them. There was no telling if they would have to start riding again right away, but they wanted to be ready no matter what happened.

After listening for more shots and hearing none, the two became anxious to know what had happened. It was hard to even guess, but there had been too many shots for any of the posse to just be shooting deer for the evening meal. Something much more serious must have taken place.

Stanford wanted to go out and look for Clara. But to leave their hideout was taking a risk, and Lassiter pointed that out to his friend.

"I say we go out and find her anyway," Stanford said. "We can't know what's going on if we stay locked up in here."

"And what if she comes back and finds us gone?" Lassiter asked. "That wouldn't be any good."

Stanford blew out his breath, exasperated. He thought of going out to look for her and leaving Lassiter behind. But he knew it wouldn't be smart to have one of them go out and leave the other at the cabin, either. Then, if the posse somehow showed up, whoever stayed behind wouldn't have a chance.

"Our best bet is to sit tight," Lassiter offered. "If Clara has already gotten through, then our chances are good. Even if she hasn't yet, she most likely will. I can't hardly imagine they would be shooting at her."

"Well, they're shooting at somebody," Stanford said.

Lassiter and Stanford tied their horses to a tree at the edge of the meadow and continued to watch the area around the cabin from the shadows. Darkness had completely fallen, and the moon was rising over the trees, nearly full once again. It was a night where riders would have to stick to the shadows to keep from being seen.

For nearly an hour Lassiter and Stanford continued to discuss whether Clara had gotten back to her father's ranch. Stanford couldn't stand not knowing what had happened to her, and more than once Lassiter had to talk him out of being impulsive and just taking off.

Stanford was about to leave anyway when both men heard a rider coming up over the ridge that separated the cabin from the creek on the other side. Whoever was coming was riding all out.

Lassiter readied his rifle, as did Stanford. Then both men recognized Clara as she came down the last stretch of the slope toward the cabin.

They ran to the door and eyed the slope behind her for someone following, as she jumped down from her horse and rushed inside. She was out of breath and her eyes were wide with fear.

"I ran into Hardy Malone," she said. "There was shooting, and I couldn't tell what was happening. Then he came through a bunch of trees and just about ran into me. He's been chasing me ever since."

"How far behind you is he now?" Lassiter wanted to know.

"I can't say for sure, but certainly far enough that he doesn't know where I went," she said. "This red stallion is real fast."

Stanford turned to Lassiter. "Do you think he could possibly show up here?" he asked.

"I don't have any idea," Lassiter said. "But if

Malone's not with the posse now, that could mean the shooting had something to do with him.''

"I don't know what to do," Clara interjected. "But I don't want to wait here for him.''

"That's smart," Lassiter agreed. "He wouldn't be able to get to us, but he'd have a field day with the horses.''

Without discussing it further, the three of them blew out the lanterns in the cabin and hurried back outside. They ran to their horses, and after mounting, Lassiter and Stanford followed Clara along another trail that would take them back around a series of big hills and across to the other side of the divide again.

They rode at a good pace, but stopped a number of times to listen to the night sounds around them. The summer crickets were everywhere, and the rush of the creek was enough to drown out most noise, so they had little fear of giving themselves away. On the other hand, it would also mask any noise made by Malone, if he were riding somewhere nearby.

They finally decided among them that their best bet was to find the posse and take their chances. Clara felt sure she could talk her father into at least waiting with the trial until more was found out about Malone— especially now that he had chased her all over the mountains.

They followed the trail back down the creek and stopped a short distance from where they could see a camp of men, their fires burning brightly.

"Who does that look like?" Lassiter answered, knowing full well that they had run right into the posse.

"They weren't that far behind us," Stanford said.

"It's the lucky break we've needed," Lassiter said. "Clara can go down and tell them about Malone.

There's a good chance that something happened and Malone broke off from them.''

"I don't want her going in alone," Stanford said. "I'm going with her."

Lassiter shrugged. "Suit yourself. I'll wait back up here for one of you to let me know what's going on."

Lassiter relaxed in the darkness while Clara and Jack Stanford rode cautiously down into camp. Clara yelled out a number of times before riding in. From where Lassiter watched, it appeared that they were welcomed.

From where he watched, Lassiter saw Johnny Ridge and the boy from the livery stable, Chelsie Burns, talking to Clara and Jack Stanford. He realized then that it would be all right for him to go down. It worried him some that he could not see Trace McCord, but then, Malone was obviously not among the posse either.

Lassiter mounted his horse. Partway down he was met by Chelsie.

"Mr. Lassiter?" he heard the boy's voice calling. "Mr. Lassiter, where are you?"

Lassiter answered, and Chelsie then told him he was now welcome to come down into camp. While they rode, Chelsie told the stories of what had happened during the day with Malone. Lassiter was interested to hear about the Box Y hands finding Curly's body. That pinned one murder on Malone, and when Malone bolted on his horse, everyone realized he had killed Allen Hutton as well.

"How does it feel to be a free man once again, Mr. Lassiter?" Chelsie asked.

Lassiter nodded. "I've got to tell you, I can rest a whole lot easier this way."

"Are you still going to ride in the race, Mr. Lassiter?" Chelsie asked.

"That depends on what Mr. Stanford wants," Lassiter answered. "I came to this valley to ride for him. If he still wants me to, I guess I will."

"It's only two days until it starts," Chelsie said. "There's a train leaving from town tomorrow afternoon. Is your horse ready for it?"

"I know he's ready to run," Lassiter said. "I've just got to get the go-ahead from Jack Stanford."

"It sure would be nice to have that money," Chelsie said.

"A lot of people are thinking that," Lassiter told him. "It's going to be a mad scramble all the way."

"Do you think Jack Stanford will want you to ride, or will he just want to see if Clara will go back to liking him again?" Chelsie asked.

"I don't know how to answer that, Chelsie," Lassiter said with a grin. "That's something you'll have to ask Jack Stanford yourself."

"Do you like Miss Clara as much as he does?"

"I like her, but in a different way," Lassiter replied. "Jack wants her to marry him."

"I guess everybody's already known that for a long time," Chelsie said. "And when Allen Hutton went to work for the Box Y, there was a lot of talk about why Clara left Jack Stanford. They talked about it all the time in the livery stable."

"I suppose they did," Lassiter said.

Lassiter got down into camp with Chelsie and drank coffee with the men in the posse, hearing again the story about Malone and what he had done. There was no reason now to stay, and the men talked of leaving right away for town or for their respective ranches.

Everyone noticed that Jack Stanford and Clara were at the edge of camp and that they seemed to be having a serious talk. There weren't many who wondered if those two weren't trying to decide what they really felt about each other.

But everyone was in a hurry to get back to town. The men saddled up and the fires were put out. Lassiter and Chelsie helped Johnny onto his horse, and while the main body of the posse rode on ahead, they stayed back to ride slower with Johnny. The ride was going to be a hard one, but Johnny felt he was extremely lucky to be alive.

They were soon joined by Clara and Jack Stanford, who had finished their talk and were headed for town. It was Stanford who first brought up the upcoming horse race.

"We've got to get over to Rock Springs and get you entered," he told Lassiter. "We've got a lot of time for you to get some rest and then catch the train tomorrow afternoon. That money could mean a lot to my operation."

Lassiter nodded. "I expected you to want to go ahead with the race. I'm ready."

"Don't be so certain he's going to win, Jack," Clara said quickly. "I'm entering Allen's horse, you know."

"I thought you said you'd think about it, and maybe back out," Stanford said. "We just discussed that."

"I know we did, Jack," she said. "And I've thought about it. I want to ride in the race."

Stanford became silent and sullen again. Though Johnny Ridge was weak from his wound, he couldn't help but laugh.

"I'm glad I'm not in love," he said. "It sure makes life complicated."

Both Clara and Jack Stanford didn't see the humor,

but Lassiter had to chuckle with Johnny. There was a lot of truth to it in most cases; but in the case of Clara and Stanford, there was no doubt about it.

Clara was as determined to ride as Stanford was not to have her ride. The more he wanted her to reconsider, the more she was certain of her decision. Finally, he told Lassiter he was going to ride on ahead to the ranch and get some things in order. He was too angry to stay with her any longer.

Finally, Clara took a trail that branched off, leading to the Box Y ranch. She wanted to rest the red stallion and get some sleep before boarding the train the following day for Rock Springs.

As Lassiter rode with Johnny and Chelsie, they discussed the race and the certain friction that would be present between Lassiter and Clara.

"How do you intend to ride for Jack Stanford against Clara?" Johnny wondered. "That's going to make enemies of everybody."

"Jack hired me to ride for him a long time ago," Lassiter replied. "He didn't tell me anything about Clara or Allen Hutton, or any of this. All I know is, there's going to be a hard cross-country race in just a few days, and I've got to get myself and my horse ready for it."

"I wanted to ride too," Johnny said. "But I guess it wasn't meant to be." He thought a moment. "What if Stanford's right and her father won't let her ride?"

"He won't be able to stop her," Lassiter said. "She's too determined."

"That's not going to set well with him," Johnny said.

Lassiter nodded. "If you feel up to it, you can come

to the train depot tomorrow when everyone's loading up their horses. Clara will be there and so will Trace McCord." He chuckled. "Maybe there'll be some fireworks that go off a little early, do you think?"

"Could be," Johnny said with a laugh. "There's been a lot already, but I think they're just beginning."

16

IT WAS NEARLY DAWN when Lassiter took the time to get some rest. He spent most of the day at Jack Stanford's ranch, sleeping and feeding his stallion. The only good thing he could think of about being chased by the posse was that the stallion had gotten a workout for the big race.

Stanford couldn't rest much and decided to go into town and see what was happening. He returned later with the news that Trace McCord had called a town-council meeting to get rid of Frank Lund. It seemed Lund didn't want to act in his position as marshal to go after Hardy Malone, or to help keep peace during the upcoming Fourth of July celebration.

Lund was still complaining about the crack on the head that Lassiter had given him. But McCord seemed to know that Lund just didn't want to have to face Lassiter and Jack Stanford, now that they were out of jail and would remain that way.

So there was a hunt on for a new marshal. Stanford

told Lassiter that Lund had already left town and McCord wanted the town council to appoint someone before the horse race ended. There would be a lot of rabble-rousing and celebration when that happened.

And there was the matter of Hardy Malone. He would have to be caught. There was no way of knowing where he was, but a posse would have to be put together to look for him.

"Why don't you put in for the job, Jack?" Lassiter asked him. "You'd be good at it. You never really did like punching cattle for a living."

Stanford shrugged. "I don't think Trace McCord could hardly promote someone he had just earlier this spring called a horse thief, do you?"

It was Lassiter's turn to shrug. "Who knows? Maybe even Trace McCord can admit he's wrong once in a while."

"We've got to get you to that train," Stanford then said. "Nothing else is really all that important right now, not until that race is over. If you win, we'll just both retire. How does that sound?"

Lassiter laughed. "I could use a little retirement right about now."

It was early evening when Lassiter and Stanford arrived in Cheyenne. During the ride, Stanford's thoughts had taken a turn, and he was wishing now there wasn't going to be a race.

"The way this is turning out, I would just as soon the Fourth of July didn't come this year," he told Lassiter, revealing his true feelings. "I couldn't persuade Clara to give up riding for anything."

"She's determined," Lassiter agreed. "But maybe she'll reconsider at the last minute."

Stanford turned in the saddle. His grin was cynical. "Sure, and maybe they'll call off the race. That's the only way she'll decide not to board the train for Rock Springs. You know that."

"Just trying to give you some hope, Jack," Lassiter told him. "I know you can't ride three hard days, because of your injuries, or you'd be out there with her. But you'll just have to trust that she's going to make the run all right."

They rode in silence to the depot. The train stood waiting, while men loaded their horses and saddles into the boxcars. There were a lot of people from all points in every direction, loading up for the trip to Rock Springs.

Extra boxcars and extra passenger cars had been brought in from Omaha to take care of the demand. There were riders from every neighboring state, who had come for their chance at the prize money. The purse had become so large that it was now being divided between the first three finishers. Fully seventy percent went to the winner, with twenty percent to second place and ten to third place.

It was certainly a lot more lucrative to come in first, and that's what everyone who was entering expected to do. What was now being called the Great Horse Race was fast becoming a major regional event.

The train continued to sit and puff while passengers crowded aboard. It would be a long push over the mountains and across the expanse of dry country they called the Red Desert. But everyone was filled with the excitement of the event, and there were few who worried or complained.

Lassiter saw Clara carrying a bucket of oats into one of the boxcars to feed the red stallion. He led his black stallion up the plank and into the same car. Stanford waited outside to greet Trace McCord as he walked toward the train to find his daughter.

Clara noticed Lassiter beside her in the boxcar, tying his stallion. She glanced at him and continued feeding the red stallion.

"I suppose you're going to ask me not to ride too," she said.

"That's not up to me, Clara," Lassiter told her. "I wish you good luck."

"What has Jack told you about us?" she wanted to know. "Has he said anything?"

"That's between you and Jack," Lassiter said. "I know he's concerned about you being in the race. But I think that's good, not bad. That means he cares a lot for you."

Lassiter knew Clara felt every bit as strongly for Stanford. That first day, when she had taken them into hiding, had made him wonder if Clara had ever really had the feelings for Allen Hutton that she had had for Stanford. Likely not, Lassiter had thought. He concluded that the sole reason she had decided to marry Allen Hutton was because of her father—a man who treasured money and position.

Allen Hutton had certainly brought that with him to the valley. It would have impressed Trace McCord and likely made him decide that this young man would be good for his daughter, and his own position.

Knowing this, and knowing that Clara didn't really have her heart in running the race, Lassiter decided it was time that he bluntly tell her what he thought. He felt it was for her own good. She might become angry and defensive, but at least she would think about it.

"I'm not so sure Allen's memory is all that important right now," he said to her. "Why don't you ask yourself if he really would want you in this race, or if you're just feeling guilty."

Clara looked at him and her eyes flashed. "What in

the world are you talking about, Mr. Lassiter?'' she asked.

"How you run your life is your business," Lassiter told her. "But it's my feeling that you decided to leave Jack Stanford and go with Allen Hutton because your father wanted it that way. Isn't that the way it was?''

The anger in Clara's eyes deepened. ''What a thing to say! How dare you!''

"You know I mean you no offense," Lassiter said. He knew it wouldn't cool her down, but he wanted her to face the facts, and so he added, ''I just don't want you taking unnecessary chances in this race because of something you think you owe Allen Hutton.''

"What I feel is none of your concern," Clara told Lassiter bluntly. ''Besides, aren't you just telling me all this on behalf of Jack? Did he put you up to this?''

"He would be mad as a hornet if he knew I was discussing this with you," Lassiter told her honestly. "I took it upon myself.''

"I wonder," she said. "You think a great deal of him, and you certainly can tell what we had between us.''

"Yes, I can tell," Lassiter admitted. "Everyone can see that. But those feelings are something you and Jack have to get figured out.''

"So why the sermon?'' she asked.

"This is going to be a dog-eat-dog, hard-fought race—right down to the very last mile," Lassiter pointed out. "Your heart's not in it and that can make it dangerous. I just think you should look inside yourself and decide how you really feel. Just face it and let what's happened pass on. You and Jack have your whole lives ahead of you.''

"Well, I think it's quite time you minded your own business, Mr. Lassiter," Clara then said. ''And I would thank you to leave me alone from here on out and not bother me during this race. We are, of course, riding against each other. I want you to keep that in mind.''

Hardy Malone rested his horse in the junipers above Porter Draw. His horse was played out from riding hard, and Malone knew he was going to have to come up with a plan if was going to be able to get himself out of the mess he was now in.

He looked from the junipers—down at the crossing where he had shot Allen Hutton—and thought of the gunfighter dressed in black who had made things so very difficult for him. Things would all be tied up in a neat package now if Lassiter hadn't showed up that day.

That man had brought him from a position of respect in the valley all the way down to a criminal being chased now by the law. Where he had once been an admired new cowhand, he was now a fugitive. Lassiter had completely reversed his fortunes.

Malone knew he could no longer get anyone to believe that Lassiter had killed Allen Hutton. All that had changed the night the stable boy had come to the posse camp with news that Curly's body had been found. When he had shot Johnny Ridge and escaped, everyone knew he had killed at least one man— Curly—and likely Allen Hutton as well.

Malone now cursed himself for not having been more careful with Curly's body. Hitting the sleeping man over the head in the bunkhouse while he slept had been easy enough, as had getting him over his horse and into the darkness of the hills behind the ranch. And the pillow had muffled the pistol shot to Curly's head.

But his mistake had been in not taking the time to bury the body properly. He had left the body covered with loose rocks, intending to come back and finish the job in the daylight so that the coyotes and prairie wolves wouldn't get to it. But he just hadn't thought it that important. Obviously someone had discovered the body after the wolves and coyotes had found it.

Malone realized that dwelling on all that now wasn't going to change his predicament. He knew he had to get out of the area, and fast. He had his chance now— just ride out while everyone was concentrating on the big race. He could go up into the gold fields of Montana Territory and likely never have to own up to what had happened down here. Or he could ride into Nevada or California and not have to worry for sure.

But there was something he decided he needed to do first—and that was to get Lassiter.

Nothing would make him rest no matter how far away he got and how safe he felt from what had happened in this valley. It gnawed at him that the gunfighter dressed in black had spoiled all his plans. He would need to settle that matter before he rode on.

But getting the gunfighter was something that wouldn't be at all easy. Malone knew everyone was watching for him now—especially Lassiter. He would not make himself an easy target along the trail the race took, that was certain.

Malone realized there was only one way that Lassiter might relax and concentrate solely on the race. And that would be to make him think that he had been taken into custody and was no longer out in hiding, no longer out waiting to ambush him somewhere along the trail.

With new confidence, Hardy Malone began to devise a plan. It was a plan that was most certain to work—if he could pull it off right. But he would need to hurry, for darkness was nearly upon him and he needed sufficient time to get back down into Cheyenne. Then he would have his revenge for sure.

17

THE TIME FOR DEPARTURE to Rock Springs was getting closer, and Lassiter knew he should be getting himself settled in one of the passenger cars. He finished rubbing down his black stallion and watched Clara finish with the red stallion in angry silence.

Lassiter knew he had likely said too much to her about Jack Stanford. She let the red stallion finish the oats in the bucket, then turned and left the boxcar. Lassiter followed, hoping her anger toward him would not last.

Outside the boxcar Lassiter joined Jack Stanford and Trace McCord. He could see that McCord had been discussing Clara's decision to race with Stanford and was anxious about it. He could also detect a feeling of new confidence in his friend, something that had not been evident before when Stanford was in Trace McCord's presence. Lassiter also noted the new depth of respect McCord had for Stanford. They had

obviously been talking about other things besides
Clara.

"Jack has offered to take the position of marshal,
vacated by Frank Lund," McCord told Lassiter.
"We're going over to where the city council is meeting
to discuss it. I believe I'll recommend him."

"You couldn't find a better man," Lassiter told
McCord.

"I believe you're right," McCord said. "I now
understand a lot more about what happened this
spring."

Clara blushed and turned away. Lassiter took his
friend's hand and shook it.

"Congratulations, Jack. I'm sure you'll be good at
the job."

"Once he's sworn in, Jack's going to organize a
posse to go after Malone," McCord continued.
"Johnny Ridge is resting from his shoulder wound,
but wants to become a main deputy. There'll be a few
others who aren't in the race who can sign up too.
Maybe we can catch Malone before the race gets to
the mountains and comes down toward town."

"We're certainly going to try," Stanford said confi-
dently.

There was a hint of warmth in Clara's eyes, but she
turned away again when she saw her father looking at
her.

"I guess there's no point in my asking one more
time if you'll pull out, is there, Clara?" he said.

"Please, Father, you know my reasons for entering."

McCord nodded. "I just wanted to try one more
time, that's all."

McCord fidgeted a moment, then stepped forward.
Clara went into his arms, and he wished her good luck.

Then he turned away and asked Lassiter to join him for a short walk.

A short ways away, while Clara and Jack talked alone, McCord turned to face Lassiter.

"I know that this will seem forward of me, especially after the way I've treated you," he said. "But I sure would appreciate it if you would watch Clara for me."

"I'll do what I can before the race begins," Lassiter promised. "But once the race is under way, she's on her own."

"I wouldn't expect you to jeopardize your own position on her behalf," McCord said. "I'm just not happy about her taking her life in her hands like that."

"She can take her care of herself," Lassiter told him. "I think you know that well enough by now."

"Yes, I know that for a fact," McCord said. "But my main concern is that Hardy Malone is loose out there somewhere. And I don't know if we can find him before the race begins."

"Don't you think he's likely left the country by now?" Lassiter asked. "What would he have to stick around for?"

"He's an unpredictable man, Lassiter," McCord said. "Nobody really knows what he's going to do."

The train began blowing its whistle, and the conductor called for all passengers to board. Lassiter watched the expression on McCord's face deepen with concern.

"I'll try and keep Clara within eyesight as much as possible," Lassiter told McCord just before he turned back for the train. "I'm sure that red stallion will be right up there among the leaders."

McCord nodded and walked across to Frank Lund's office.

With a lot of talking and laughing among the passengers, the train finally pulled out. The aisles were filled with people moving about, and each passenger car was loaded.

Clara had found a seat near the front of one of the cars, and Lassiter sat down beside her. He would stick close to Clara, as he had promised Trace McCord. Though he knew she didn't like the idea, she would have to get used to it, for he didn't intend to break his word to her father.

Lassiter could see that the relationship between Trace McCord and his daughter had reached a crossroads. Clara had made a lot of promises to her father over the years—Allen Hutton having been one of them. McCord certainly wanted the best for his daughter, and she, in turn, had tried to make him happy.

But she was changing now. Lassiter could plainly see that she wanted to make some decisions about her life on her own now—even if she was out in the middle of the frontier.

It had been a big step for Clara to ride off at dawn to help two fugitives her father wanted caught. And now, to run in the horse race despite Trace McCord's disapproval, was another big leap—possibly even bigger than the first one.

As the train moved on, Lassiter pulled out a map of the course they were to ride during the race and began to study it. The race would cover some two hundred fifty miles, none of it easy. Lassiter knew the course well, for he had taken the same trail across from Utah to come to Cheyenne.

It was a rugged trail that started in the open ravines of sagebrush and greasewood around Rock Springs and then continued east across an expanse of territory they called the Red Desert. From there it wound up into the mountains—the Medicine Bow range—and then down the other side and into Cheyenne. A hard trip for even the best of horses and men.

There were to be five major check-in stations along the way. Two of them were stage stops on the Red Desert, and the third was at Bridger Pass, just west of the Medicine Bow range.

The fourth one was a fort that was mostly deserted, but still being maintained as a residence or main line camp for some of the big cattle companies. Fort Halleck had served its short time when the railroad had come through.

Along the trail between the third and fourth check-in points was a steep slope that went for nearly two hundred yards almost straight downhill. This spot was without question the most dangerous part of the race.

The last check-in point was Fort Sanders, near the booming town of Laramie. From there the last fifty miles of the race would bring the winner to the screaming crowd waiting at the celebration in Cheyenne.

"Whoever gets to Fort Sanders first has a good chance of winning the race," Lassiter pointed out to Clara.

Clara nodded halfheartedly. She glanced at the map and then back out the window. Lassiter realized she was tired, but there was also something else to blame for her lack of enthusiasm.

"What's the matter?" he asked her. "Did you decide you don't want to ride this race after all?"

Clara turned to him and frowned. "I wouldn't be here if I didn't."

Lassiter shrugged. "I just thought you weren't especially sociable."

"I told you when we were feeding the horses in the

boxcar that we aren't going to be friends on this trip," Clara said bluntly. "Or don't you remember that?"

"I just thought you might change your mind," Lassiter said.

Clara frowned again. "Well, I haven't. And I don't particularly relish the idea of you babysitting me either. I realize my father doesn't want me riding and that you promised you'd keep an eye out for me, but I don't have to pretend to be a child."

"I guess I understand," Lassiter said. "But I don't believe I've been treating you as a child."

"I'm really not in the mood to discuss things, Mr. Lassiter," she said. "I need some rest so that I'll be ready for the race when we get to Rock Springs. It's for certain there won't be a lot of time for a good rest once the race gets under way."

Lassiter nodded. He watched as Clara turned toward the window and lay her head on the back of the seat. He continued to study the map until he heard a voice in the aisle beside him.

"Mr. Lassiter, I finally found you."

It was Chelsie Burns, and his eyes were wide.

"What are you doing here, Chelsie?" Lassiter asked.

"I'm hoping to enter the race," he answered. "What else?"

Lassiter looked at him a moment. "You don't know what you're getting yourself into, Chelsie."

Chelsie nodded. "Oh, yes I do. I'm not riding to win; Pa doesn't have the money to enter me. But I just want to be on the trail and see what happens."

"It's too dangerous for just a Sunday ride, Chelsie," Lassiter warned him. "You could be hurt, or even killed."

Again Chelsie shook his head. "No, I've got a little

buckskin that's as tough as nails. He's fast and he's durable. I won't be in any trouble."

"I'm trying to say," Lassiter continued, "there's no telling what can happen out there. The country's rough and hot and dry. It's going to be hard for even those who are used to it."

Chelsie smiled. "You just don't want me to beat you, do you, Mr. Lassiter? I can understand that."

Lassiter had to laugh. "I guess I don't, Chelsie. And if there's anyone who can do it, I'd bet it will be you."

Chelsie smiled from ear to ear and nodded. "I wish you good luck, Mr. Lassiter. May the best man win."

Lassiter took Chelsie's hand when he extended it and shook it. He watched the boy then twist his way down the aisle and into another car.

Lassiter then leaned back against the seat and adjusted his hat over his eyes. He was going to try and get some sleep, despite all the noise. But all he could think about was the kid, Chelsie Burns, and his big smile of confidence.

It made Lassiter smile to himself. It was true—if anyone else had the heart to make it all the way and win, it was that kid. And it wouldn't be a big surprise if he did just that.

Cheyenne was settled and peaceful, but an odd state of affairs lingered in town. The reason was that most of the men were on the train headed for Rock Springs, and mostly old-timers had been left behind to keep the saloon lights glowing.

The situation was perfect for Hardy Malone, who tied his horse in the darkness in an alley behind the telegraph office. There was no one to speak of anywhere to be seen, but he moved cautiously anyway.

He had learned something from past mistakes, and he couldn't afford not to have this final plan work for him now.

Malone looked both ways, then pulled his gun at the door to the telegraph office. There was but a single lantern glowing inside, and the elderly man who ran the office was asleep on a bunk in the back. Malone saw that it would even be easier than he had first imagined.

No longer trying to be silent, Malone burst through the door and over to the bunk. The old man awoke with a start and tried to cover his head with the blankets. Malone pulled them down, and the old man, his teeth chattering, put his hands out in front of him, begging Malone not to shoot.

"Just get up and do what I tell you," Malone said. "Then we'll see what happens."

"What do you want of me?" the old man asked, sitting up in his bunk.

"You're going to send a message for me to the marshal in Rock Springs," Malone told him. "Now, get over to your telegraph."

The old man climbed out from under the blankets and stumbled across the floor in his long underwear. Malone looked out one of the windows to be sure no one was coming, then went to where the old man had seated himself at the telegraph.

"There might be no one there," the old man said.

"Don't give me that!" Malone hissed. "Work that thing until someone answers. And you'd better not pull anything."

The old man broke the line to Rock Springs and worked his telegraph until he got somebody up to take the message. He looked to Malone, who then dictated these words:

Alert to marshal of Rock Springs Stop Hardy Malone has surrendered Stop Repeat Hardy Malone has given himself up and is in jail at Cheyenne Stop Cancel all warrants Stop Trace McCord Stop End of message Stop

"Did that get through?" Malone asked the old man.

"Yes, they got it," the old man said.

"Are you sure?"

"Yes, I promise," the old man said. "I'll have them verify what they recorded."

The old man worked the telegraph and got the reply that they had indeed gotten the message in Rock Springs and were going to relay it to the marshal right away. Malone looked at the message of dots and dashes on the paper and nodded. Then he told the old man to turn the telegraph off.

"What for?" the old man asked. "I ain't going to send nothing more."

"Just turn it off," Malone said angrily.

The look in Malone's eyes scared the old man again, and he quickly unhooked the telegraph where the wires from outside connected.

"I don't want to hear any more out of you, or you're dead, old man," Malone then threatened him. "Got that?"

The old man nodded feebly. He watched while Malone began pounding the telegraph keys, bending them, and snapping some of them off with the butt of his pistol. The old man's mouth opened but he didn't say a word.

Finally, Malone seemed satisfied and ushered the old man away from the desk and back to his bunk.

"You ain't going to shoot me now, are you?" the

old man pleaded. "I ain't going to say nothing to nobody. I promise."

"I know you're not," Malone said. "Because it's going to be a long time before you even remember what happened here tonight—if you ever do."

Malone slammed the barrel of his revolver into the old man's head and watched him sigh and fall back onto the bunk. He hit him twice more, to be sure the old man wouldn't recover for a long time. If the old man died, that really didn't matter; there had been no gunshots to alert anybody.

Malone then hurried out the door and into the night once again. He climbed onto his horse and rode slowly out of town, keeping to the shadows so as not to make noise or be seen by any wandering passersby.

Once safely out of town, Malone kicked his horse into a run and followed the trail in the moonlight which would take him up into the Medicine Bow mountains. He had already decided just where to wait for Lassiter. He was going to settle things with the gunfighter dressed in black once and for all.

18

IT WAS JUST AFTER SUNRISE, July first, and Rock Springs was filled with anxious men and women, all a part of the overland race that would end in Cheyenne during the celebration on the Fourth. Everywhere the riders readied their horses and looked over the competition, eager to begin.

Everyone knew the rules, for there were any number of sheets tacked up at the railway station and all over town. Unlike some races, where a number of horses were used and the rider was the winner, the horse was marked with the number. It was the horse that would have to meet the challenge and come in first, not the rider.

That was the reason Lassiter felt he had as good or better chance than anyone else at taking first place. He knew his horse very well and how to pace the animal over a long distance. He had run from enough men chasing him that both he and his stallion knew instinctively how to make the most miles over the shortest period of time.

He was certainly not taking Clara lightly, though. She was determined, and the red stallion she was riding had a lot of stamina. Lassiter knew it would be close to the very end.

The race was set to begin in but a few minutes. Clara looked distressed as she took last-minute glances at the map of the route, which included the check-in points along the way. She seemed a lot friendlier than when she had first boarded the train, and Lassiter wondered if she didn't finally realize he wasn't trying to hold her back from the race.

"I didn't mean all those things I said to you last night," she told him. "I'm sorry."

"Don't worry about it," Lassiter said. "You're under a heavy load of stress, what with worrying about all that's going on."

Lassiter knew that she was now concerning herself with the fact that her father had actually made Stanford the new marshal. His assignment was going to be a dangerous one, possibly more dangerous than when he had been a fugitive on the run.

"Malone's certain to be along the way somewhere, just waiting to ambush you," she said. "Do you really *have* to be in this race?"

Lassiter suddenly realized that she had been thinking about his safety too. Clara had realized that Malone was going to blame him personally for all that had gone wrong.

"I promised Jack I'd run it for him," Lassiter said. "I can't back out on that now. He's paid the entry fee and everything."

Lassiter sat his black stallion next to Clara on her red and waited for the starter to make the announcement for the competitors to take their marks. Even though the morning sun was brand new, the day promised to be hot once again. It would be a long ride.

While he waited for the race to begin, he noticed Chelsie Burns riding toward him through the crowd. When Chelsie finally got through, Lassiter said, "I thought you said you were going along for fun, not to race."

"I am," Chelsie said quickly, with a nod. "But there's some news going around that I thought you should hear."

Chelsie then told both Lassiter and Clara about the telegraph that had reached the marshal late the night before.

"The word's all around that Jack Stanford caught Malone," Chelsie finished. "He's in jail back in Cheyenne. The telegraph was sent by Trace McCord himself."

Lassiter looked to Clara, who seemed relieved. He took a deep breath himself; though it had seemed like a long shot to catch Malone right away, he was happy that his friend had managed a lucky break.

"That takes our mind off one big problem," Lassiter said. "I guess the race is the main thing now."

Clara nodded. "May the best horse win."

Lassiter laughed. "Yeah, and no fair feeding that red stallion oats along the way. He has to win on just grass."

"He will," Clara promised.

The race got under way, the throng of riders beginning the long run across the rough and rugged trail to Cheyenne. Dust boiled up over Rock Springs like a huge thunderhead. Most had started all out, hoping for a good lead.

But Lassiter didn't worry about the pace. He kept

his stallion at a steady gallop and tried to keep out of the way when other riders raced past him. He knew their horses would soon be tiring and their riders would all be walking before long.

Soon Lassiter lost sight of Chelsie and Clara in the surging rush of riders. The contestants were like an immense herd of rushing power that thundered across the open expanses toward the mountains to the east. Most anything could happen, Lassiter thought, and at any time.

But in the end he knew Clara and Chelsie would be among the strongest left to run the last hard miles into Cheyenne.

Jack Stanford walked into the jail and took a few minutes to look around and get his mind straightened out. Things had changed a lot since his last time in this building. He'd been a prisoner then, breaking free with Lassiter. It was now a shock to come in as the new marshal.

It took him a while to get used to it. He had to fight the intense anger he felt, remembering what Frank Lund had done to him. His ribs were still swollen and sore, but they were healing. And his head had finally cleared and the persistent headaches had let up.

Frank Lund was gone now, and there was nothing left but the empty inside of the jail. A new lock would have to be installed in the cell door, as the old one had been pried apart to get into Lund after Lassiter had struck him on the head with his own pistol.

And a new desk would have to be ordered, Stanford thought to himself. He had a mind to set a match right away to the one that had Frank Lund's initials scratched in the top.

But none of it bothered Stanford so much that he

wasn't glad he was the new marshal. He decided that he didn't have time to contemplate the past and the future, as there were a number of men waiting for him to join them. His new job was to enforce the law, and he would do whatever it took.

He had organized a posse to look for Malone. They would go west into the mountains and meet with the marshal from Rock Springs and a group he was bringing with him. They had wired back and forth the afternoon before to set it all up.

The two posses would unite, and if either hadn't run into Malone along the way, they would set up guard posts along the trail where the race was to be run. If Malone didn't show up by the time the race was over, they could assume he was no longer around.

They had sent out warrants, and Wanted posters were to be printed. But as far as Stanford was concerned now, it was a waste of time. Likely, Malone was long gone into the next territory and nobody would ever see him again. He could see nothing now that would keep Malone around—unless there was something he hadn't thought of yet.

Stanford was finding himself a rifle and some ammunition to join the posse when Trace McCord burst through the door.

"Malone's been at the telegraph office," he said. "Must have been sometime late last night. Old Sherman Straub is dead—his head bashed in. One of my hands was going in to send a telegraph not long ago and found him."

Stanford stood numbed with shock. "Malone? How do you know for sure it was him?"

"The hand found the telegraph machine completely ruined," McCord answered. "And he also found this."

McCord handed Stanford a copy of a telegraph that had been lying on the floor. It was a false statement sent to the marshal at Rock Springs, claiming that Malone had been caught and was in the Cheyenne jail.

Stanford read it and looked up at McCord. "I suppose the law over there has called off the search for Malone now. They likely think he's in jail and there's nothing to worry about."

"It looks that way," McCord said. "I guess we're on our own. And my daughter's up there on that crazy ride."

"Malone's got a big head start on us," Stanford pointed out. "Too big to make up with a posse. When's the next train out of here?"

"Not until late this afternoon," McCord said. "I don't know if I can stand to wait that long."

"The race can't possibly get as far as Laramie before tomorrow night," Stanford said, thinking as fast as he could. "If we take the posse and ride the train there, we can fan out in all directions. That way we'll be there when Clara shows up."

McCord took a deep breath. "Maybe that's a good idea. But I'm going to take some of my hands and ride to the mountains from here. I can't stand waiting. Maybe we'll luck out and run into Malone before he gets as far as Laramie."

Stanford nodded. "I wish there was some way to get word over to Rock Springs. But I guess we'll have to do it all ourselves."

McCord turned and fairly ran out of the office. Stanford grabbed the rifle and ammunition and rushed after him, feeling every bit as keyed up. Clara meant just as much to him as she could to anybody, and he didn't want anything to happen to her.

* * *

The race went on across the Red Desert country, the heat mounting with each passing minute.

Midday approached, and as Lassiter had predicted, the heat began to take its toll on the inexperienced riders. At the first check-in at the Rock Point Stage Station, Lassiter found himself passing a number of riders who were drinking water heavily and trying to rest their already-weary horses.

He saw both Chelsie and Clara not far ahead of him. They were riding close to one another and making good time across the expanse of red dust and rock.

Neither Lassiter nor his horse took much water at the stop, but continued on across the open expanse of red countryside. Midday passed and brought even worse scorching heat. Lassiter removed an extra bandana from his saddlebag and used it to cover his stallion's head. He had saturated the bandana at the check-in point, and the cool wetness helped the horse to cope with the intense heat.

Lassiter caught up with Clara and Chelsie at the second check-in point, the Le Clede Stage Station. It was getting late in the day, and though there were still a lot of riders ahead of them, Lassiter knew the next day would take its toll on even more of those in the race.

They had nearly crossed the worst of the day's course. The Red Desert was as formidable a ride this time of year as anyplace on the Northern Plains. Chelsie was holding up incredibly well, as was Clara. Lassiter wasn't so surprised about Clara, but he couldn't imagine a boy of Chelsie's age having the reserve and determination to go through a grinding ride like this one.

True to his word, though, Chelsie was riding a good horse. More like an Indian pony, the animal wasn't nearly as fast as his black stallion or Clara's red, but the tough little buckskin had stamina enough for a whole herd and could keep up a good pace over a very long distance.

They camped that night on Bitter Creek, in a high shelf of hills east of the Dug Springs Stage Station. Though it was still dry country and covered with dust and sagebrush, it was higher in elevation than the surrounding desert. This would afford the horses better rest and a cooler night.

Many of the riders, Lassiter knew, had pushed their horses as far as Sulfur Spring, hoping to outdistance the competition the first day. But it didn't work that way. Their tired horses would be reluctant to push themselves up over Bridger Pass the following day.

Over an open fire, Lassiter warmed up a supply of beans and dried venison that he had brought with him. At the edge of camp a small pack of coyotes watched, while the three of them sat around the fire and talked about the rest of the race.

Lassiter was looking at the map again, studying it and getting an idea in his mind of how long it was going to take to reach Cheyenne ahead of everyone else, realizing how hard that was going to be.

"There's a lot of fast horses in this race," Chelsie said. "I hope they don't all hold up."

"By late evening tomorrow, we'll be in higher country," Lassiter said. "It will be a lot easier on the horses, and we can go faster. Those who pushed too hard down here on the desert will have trouble high up in the mountains."

"I wish we were at Laramie already," Clara said. "This race would then be a lot closer to being over."

"Yeah," Chelsie said. "But then we'd be at that big

dropoff in the trail. I'm not looking forward to riding down that."

"You don't have to ride down that," Lassiter said. "You're not in this race. That would be risking your life for no reason."

"I'm not going all the way around and lose you two," Chelsie said. "I'll take my chances on the slope."

Lassiter watched him crawl into his blankets, as did Clara. They were both dead tired, as was he. But the race was hardly started.

Though they had gotten across most of the desert, they had the mountains, the final drive past Laramie, the big slope, and then the hills to Cheyenne still ahead of them. It would take them over two more days of hard riding and few stops. He worried about Clara and Chelsie; a lot could happen between now and then.

19

HARDY MALONE HAD MADE cold camp for two days in a deep canyon just off the main trail. He felt safe and confident here. The riders would come past during the race, and it was a good place to set up an ambush for Lassiter.

The spot was just down the trail a ways from where the big slope ended. There was certain to be a lot of confusion after that part of the race—just enough to make Lassiter an easy target.

He had been sorely tempted to start shooting early, for a posse led by Jack Stanford and Trace McCord had come by earlier in the day. They were no doubt looking for him, and it made him nervous. But he was well hidden and he was sure they wouldn't find him.

He had thought about the posse, and couldn't understand why he hadn't seen Frank Lund. Unless Lund had some other men looking in other parts of the mountains, he should have been with them. Malone didn't think it really mattered anyway, as he was after

Lassiter. He wanted the gunfighter dressed in black dead more than anything else in the world.

As he often had since arriving two days prior, Malone took a seat under a large pine in the area below where the trail snaked through. He was there once again, looking, when he spotted a lone rider coming up.

He watched carefully as the rider continued to work his horse along the trail. Malone grunted when he realized the rider was Frank Lund.

He hurried back to his horse and pulled his rifle. Then he mounted and rode to where a patch of timber grew just back from the trail. He watched to see if anyone was following Lund, then waited until Lund was close enough that he couldn't get away.

Malone then rode out of the trees.

"Just hold it there, Lund," he ordered.

Lund made no attempt at all to escape, but threw up his hands with a smile.

"I've been looking for you," he said.

"I'll bet you have," Malone replied. "But you're crazy to come alone."

"You don't understand," Lund said. "I'm not the marshal anymore."

Malone was surprised. Then he didn't believe him.

"Is this some kind of trick?"

"No trick. McCord got the town council to fire me. That's why I was looking for you. I wanted to team up with you and maybe settle a score with McCord."

"You had better be telling me this straight," Malone said. "Otherwise you're a dead man."

"You know I wouldn't be alone if I still worked for the law," Lund said. "I'm not that stupid."

"That posse was by here earlier today," Malone said.

"I saw them too," Lund said with a nod. "I was hoping they'd pass you by."

Malone studied Lund for a while, then took both his rifle and his pistol. Lund didn't seem to mind. Malone then put his own rifle back in its scabbard.

"If you're telling the truth about all this, you won't be worrried about your guns until the race gets here," Malone told him. "You can have them back once Lassiter rides into my sights."

"Fair enough," Lund said. "Just so I get a chance to capture Clara. I'm going to make Trace McCord pay highly for making me look like a fool."

Malone nodded himself. "Come back to my camp and make yourself comfortable. We've got just over a day to wait yet. But time passes fast when you're thinking about getting somebody in your gunsights."

The last check-in point at Fort Sanders was now a half day behind Lassiter. His stallion was holding up well, as was Clara's red and the little buckskin Chelsie Burns was riding.

Dawn was breaking and they were saddling up for the last stretch through the rest of the mountains and foothills down into Cheyenne. A steady pace over the last two days had brought them out in front of the vast majority of riders. But there were still a good number up with them, and everyone was intent on winning.

Lassiter looked at the map one more time. Most of the roughest and hardest country was behind them, and now it looked like the big slope was going to tell the tale on who was really in the race. They would reach it somewhere close to noon, and those who got down that steep and treacherous piece of trail first would have a strong chance of winning it all.

Lassiter thought about their ride to this point and

hoped nothing would make things any harder for them. Heat and sparse grass along the gullies had slowed everybody up and caused any number of riders to drop out already.

When they had finally gotten up off the desert, through Bridger Pass and into the mountains, the ride had been a great deal easier in terms of food and water for the horses. From there they had been more or less enjoying themselves. The days had been long, but they were not too hot, and the nights were cool enough to give the horses good rest.

As close as it was getting to the end of the race, Lassiter knew something had to happen. As he looked out into the rising sun, he saw a group of riders coming from a different trail than the one being used for the race, and knew his intuition about trouble was coming true.

As they finished saddling, Clara's father and Jack Stanford approached with a posse of men and pulled up in a cloud of dust to tell them about Hardy Malone sending the fake telegraph message.

"That puts a whole new light on things," Lassiter said.

"It changes everything," Jack Stanford agreed.

"I want you to pull out of the race, Clara," McCord said. "It's way too dangerous now."

"I've gone this far," she protested. "I can't pull out. Besides, I'm not in that much danger."

"But you *are* in that much danger," McCord argued with her. "Malone is out here, and anything can happen."

"If you ride with me, then you'll know I'm safe," Clara said.

"You know we can't keep up with your horses," Stanford put in. "This is for your own good."

"My own good is to win this race," Clara said. "I'll do that, and everything will be fine."

"Clara, I don't want to argue with you," McCord said. "I shouldn't have even let you enter in the first place."

Clara took a deep breath, and in the early light her eyes were flashing. "Father, when are you going to learn that I'm a grown woman and capable of making my own decisions?" she said. "I've been doing what *you've* wanted for far too long. And it's caused some problems. Why can't you just let me take risks, even get myself into trouble if I want to? It's about time you let me do what *I* want for a change."

With those words she kicked the red stallion into a run. She had the horse stretched full out before anyone could even begin to go after her.

McCord and Stanford both called to her, but she kept on riding. McCord pulled his hat from his head and slapped it against his leg.

"Dammit! I can't have her out there with Malone loose. It's too dangerous."

He looked around at Lassiter and Jack Stanford, who were watching him. He knew what they were thinking—that he wasn't letting her grow up on her own.

"I guess I should have let her make more of her own decisions before," he finally said. "But right now is a fine time to have her rebel like this."

Other riders were coming up now, and Lassiter told McCord and Stanford that he would do what he could to keep her safe. Chelsie had already left on his buckskin to catch up with her, and when Lassiter left, McCord and Stanford could do little but lead the posse after them.

Lassiter rode hard to catch up with Clara and Chelsie. They were riding in a tight group with a large number of other riders who had made it this far and were determined to make the race close.

Lassiter finally moved out a short ways ahead of Clara and Chelsie, to watch for any signs of Hardy Malone. Nothing caught his eye for another two hours. Then he knew he was going to have to forget about Malone, for the hardest part of the race was now looming just ahead.

After a short drink of water at a spring, Lassiter kicked his black stallion into a run. Just ahead was the long slope which would severely test all the horses and their riders. And with so many riders going down at the same time, there was a lot of danger involved.

The dust thickened as the large group of riders spurred their horses ahead, working them into a frenzy before they reached the slope. Any horse that hesitated would either have to be turned away, out of the race, or risk being knocked off balance at the crest of the slope.

Lassiter found himself crowded on his left and right by riders eager to take the lead. Clara was just behind him, closing in with her red stallion, and Chelsie was close behind her.

When they hit the edge of the slope, Lassiter let his black jump off gently, not surge like some of the other riders were doing with their horses. That way the black kept his balance while all around him other horses were losing theirs.

The black stallion then picked up his speed and leaped down the steep slope, catching himself and bouncing ahead in stride while Lassiter held his free arm high for balance and sat as far back in the saddle as he could.

To his right a horse tumbled head over heels, throwing its rider and then rolling over him. Other horses were then caught in the spill and a pileup started.

Lassiter knew he couldn't turn to see if Clara had avoided the disaster, or he might lose his own balance. Besides, there was too much dust to really make out anyone—even if they were riding right beside him.

Lassiter's black continued down the slope, leaving the massive confusion behind. The dust continued to boil up and envelop numbers of confused riders. Lassiter could hear the cursing, yelling men and the squealing horses behind him as his black finally reached the bottom of the slope and broke away into a dead run.

A distance from the slope, where the trail broke into a flat meadow, Lassiter slowed his stallion and turned to see who had survived the rush downhill. Many men were off their horses, leading them, checking to see if they were lame. Many were, and would have to be taken out of the race.

But somehow Chelsie and his buckskin had survived. Finally, Clara and her red stallion emerged from the torrent of dust, and Lassiter could see that her horse was still running well.

Only two other men followed them, but Lassiter could see that their horses were played out completely and wouldn't last much longer. Still, there would be others along, eager to catch up, before much more time passed. There was no time to slow down.

Lassiter let Chelsie ride past him while he waited for Clara to catch up. He noticed something wrong with her, though, as she approached. She was holding her head as she rode.

Lassiter tried to get her to stop, but she insisted they go on. He didn't know what kind of injury she had sustained—possibly a rock that had struck from a flying set of hooves. Anything could have happened in a madhouse like the ride down the slope.

All Lassiter knew now was that he had to keep Clara going and somehow keep pace with Chelsie up ahead. There wasn't more than a half day left to Cheyenne, but it was going to be the hardest half day he had put in for a long time.

Malone and Lund had been watching the dust boil up from the slope. They were both on the crest, watching for Lassiter and Clara to come from the meadow and finally into the narrow part of the trail where it brushed the edge of the canyon. They didn't have long to wait, for Lassiter and Clara weren't that far away.

What they didn't expect was to see Chelsie Burns out in front. They could see the boy from the livery stable riding all out not too far in front of Clara and Lassiter. All the other riders were still a good distance behind and wouldn't see anything. The situation was perfect.

"Which one do you want?" Malone asked Lund.

"I told you, I want to capture Clara McCord," Lund said. "I don't want to shoot her. What good is she to me if she's dead?"

"Then wait until I get Lassiter before you go down for her," Malone ordered. "He's the main reason I'm going through all this. Otherwise, I'd be long gone from here by now."

Malone jumped on his horse and waited for Lund to mount also. Malone wanted to get down to the patch of trees in plenty of time to be there for a close shot when Lassiter and Clara came through. There was some open space up the trail for a ways, but the shot at the trees would be perfect.

Malone was in a hurry, and as he rode his horse along the ridge to get down to the trees, he was aware that the stable boy was just below. Some loose rock began to tumble down the hill, and the boy stopped his horse and looked up.

Malone pulled up and watched as Chelsie turned his horse around and headed back along the trail toward Lassiter and Clara, who were just riding from the meadow into the narrow part of the trail.

"Shoot him!" Lund yelled. "You've got to shoot him before he warns them."

"It's too late for that," Malone growled. "I'd better train my sights on Lassiter."

20

LASSITER WAS RIDING CLOSE to Clara, telling her she had better stop before she fell off her horse. But Clara felt she could stay on, and wanted to ride the race through until the end.

Lassiter then looked up to see Chelsie riding toward them on his buckskin as hard as he could.

"Mr. Lassiter, you've got to turn back!" he yelled. "It's Hardy Malone. He's waiting to ambush you. And Frank Lund is with him." Chelsie turned and pointed up onto the ridge above the trail.

Lassiter looked up along the ridge to see Malone and Lund both kneeling, leveling their rifles. Their shots rang out and both Lassiter and Clara leaned over in the saddle and held tight to their horses.

"Split up!" Lassiter yelled to Clara and Chelsie. "They want me, not you two."

Clara and Chelsie turned their horses for a nearby patch of timber. But Chelsie's buckskin stumbled in the rocks and went down, throwing him. Clara's red stallion leaped clear, but she stopped the horse and held onto the saddle horn to let herself down. She was woozy from her head injury.

Chelsie got up with his horse, unhurt, but the buckskin had picked up a small rock and it was lodged under the shoe on the left front foot. He couldn't ride, or the buckskin would certainly come up lame.

Clara was wobbling, holding her head, while the red stallion ran into the nearby timber. She seemed dazed and disoriented as Chelsie ran over to her.

Lassiter had already reached another growth of pine nearby, and seeing what had happened to Clara and Chelsie, turned to go back out. Chelsie was trying to help Clara, but they both were in a great deal of danger.

The reason was evident as Lassiter looked up toward the slope above the trail. Both Malone and Lund were obsessed with what they had come to do.

Lund was riding his horse as fast as he could down off the ridge, his rifle raised to shoot Chelsie. The boy was working desperately to get Clara to move toward the timber, while Lund's horse steadily gained ground.

Malone was on the ridge, getting his rifle ready for Lassiter, when he showed himself again.

Risking his own life, Lassiter pulled his rifle, rode out from the timber and through Hardy Malone's bullets toward Chelsie and Clara. He jumped down from his horse, letting the stallion run free back into the timber.

Malone fired again and again as Lassiter moved. Finally, while Malone reloaded his rifle, Lassiter took aim for a quick shot. His main concern was Lund, who was closing fast on Chelsie and Clara.

Lassiter took a quick shot at Malone on the ridge, just to scare him and keep him from shooting. The bullet nearly got Malone, whining off a rock near his left shoulder. Then Malone moved back behind the rock, giving Lassiter just enough time to train his rifle on Lund.

Lund had already shot once at Chelsie, narrowly missing him. But Chelsie was still helping Clara. He had her close to the timber now and was urging her on.

Lassiter took a deep breath and leveled his rifle. Just as Lund prepared for another shot at Chelsie, Lassiter pulled the trigger.

The blast took Lund in the right side of his chest, just next to his upper arm, and twisted him in the saddle. His rifle flew to the ground and he yelled as he fell, bouncing into the rocks.

Malone had come out from cover behind the rock on the ridge and was aiming at Lassiter, who jumped as the muzzle flashed. The bullet grazed him along the top of his shoulder, and he rolled into a prone position on the ground, bringing his rifle up and ready.

Malone was levering another round into his rifle when Lassiter fired. Malone groaned and jerked backward, flopping and rolling down the slope of rocks to the bottom. He came to his knees as Lassiter levered another round into the chamber of his rifle and hurried toward the slope.

Malone was on his feet again, his left arm hanging useless. His rifle lay up among the rocks on the slope. But he had no intention of giving himself up, and pulled his pistol. He fired wildly at Lassiter, though Lassiter was still out of effective range. Bullets whined off rocks at Lassiter's feet while he moved steadily toward Malone.

In a frantic effort to win the fight, Malone reloaded his pistol and looked up. Lassiter had stopped within twenty feet of him, holding his rifle down loosely in his left hand as he looked into Malone's crazed eyes.

Malone couldn't believe Lassiter was standing there with the rifle just hanging loose.

"You're a fool, Lassiter," he slurred. "I'm going to kill you."

"You can stop all this by just putting that pistol down," he told Malone. "Nobody else has to die."

Malone's breathing was ragged. "I don't aim to give up to you, Lassiter, now or ever!"

Malone clicked the cylinder back into position and raised the pistol to shoot. But Lassiter's hand had already closed around his revolver, and it was out of the holster and pointing at Malone.

The blast sounded and hammered Malone backward. He spun halfway around and fell onto his face in the rocks. His body tensed as the air left his lungs, and he lay still.

Lassiter turned back and hurried to where Chelsie was sitting with Clara. He had gone to the stream and had put a cold, wet cloth to her head. She was beginning to feel better, and her spirits were rising.

By now the other riders in the race were catching up. They passed without stopping. Then Jack Stanford and Trace McCord led the posse into view.

McCord jumped down from his horse, next to Clara. He did not yell, but only asked if she was all right. Jack Stanford got down just as quickly and stood with them.

"I'm fine," Clara told them both. "Thanks to these two."

Stanford made a comment about Lassiter's shoulder, saying he should pull himself out of the race.

"I'm going to," Lassiter said. "Chelsie's horse

came up lame. He can ride my stallion. It's the horse that's declared the winner anyway.''

Chelsie looked at Lassiter and his eyes widened. ''But I can't.''

''Why not?''

''He's yours.''

''I'm hurt. You ride him, Chelsie. You didn't have to come back to warn us; you could have won the race. Now, get on and ride him into Cheyenne. And get there first!''

Lassiter held the stallion for Chelsie while he jumped on, and then kicked the big black horse into a run. Jack Stanford went over with Clara to get her red stallion, while Lassiter and Trace McCord helped the men in the posse load Malone and Lund onto the backs of their horses.

Lassiter then took some time to work the rock loose from under the shoe of the buckskin. Trace McCord watched with deep admiration. Here was a man who helped people and cared little about taking the credit. He had once wanted to see this man hang, and he couldn't believe now that he had been so blind.

Jack Stanford and Clara rode over from where they had been talking, and Clara was smiling.

''Thank you, Father, for letting me make my own mistake this time,'' she said. ''Now I feel like I've made my own decision and have had to live with it.''

''That slope must have been a crazy ride,'' McCord said to her.

Clara nodded. ''Yes, but no more crazy rides like that for me. One is more than enough. Maybe a smaller slope, but not one like that again.''

Trace McCord smiled at his daughter and watched her and Jack Stanford leave for Cheyenne. Lassiter was now on the little buckskin, making sure it wasn't lame. It rode well, and he wasn't concerned about going back to town. He was in no real hurry now anyway.

"Maybe you'd better have a doctor look at that shoulder, Lassiter," McCord advised.

"I'll get by until after the victory celebration," Lassiter told him. "I'll wager you better than even money that Chelsie takes my black into Cheyenne first. He's quite a rider."

McCord smiled. "A lot of things have happened in a short time around here," he said. "I guess I've learned a few things."

"We all have," Lassiter said.

McCord nodded. "Let's head for Cheyenne. We don't want to miss the festivities."

When Lassiter reached Cheyenne with the others, Chelsie Burns was still in the winner's circle, accepting congratulations from friends. His father was talking to people, proud as any father could be, and Johnny Ridge was holding the black stallion's reins.

When Chelsie saw Lassiter, he rode the stallion over and took back his buckskin.

"I won your money for you, Mr. Lassiter," Chelsie said.

"No, that money's for you, Chelsie," Lassiter said. "You're going to put it away and save up some more, so you can go to school and get a degree and become a doctor who works with people to solve their problems. Johnny Ridge told me about your ambition."

"You think I can really be one of those special kind of doctors?" Chelsie said, his eyes wide again.

"You sure can," Lassiter said. "You can be anything you want."

"Are you going to stay here in Cheyenne?" Chelsie asked, already knowing the answer.

"I've got to move on," Lassiter told him. "But I'd bet good money we meet again some day."

"I know we will, Mr. Lassiter," Chelsie said. "And I'll look forward to it."

The Fourth of July festivities continued while Lassiter got his shoulder treated by a local doctor. He then spent some time with his friend Jack Stanford and wished him the best. Stanford told him that the job as marshal would likely be ending soon; Clara had told her father she didn't want Jack taking any more chances with his life than he had to.

As Lassiter was preparing to leave, Trace McCord came over and offered him the job as marshal.

"You've got a lifetime job here, if you want it," McCord told him. "We need men like you."

"I never was much good at staying in one place very long," Lassiter replied.

McCord shook his hand. "If you ever change your mind, you know where to come."

McCord went over to watch the greased-pig race with Jack Stanford, and Clara took the opportunity to talk to Lassiter alone.

"I guess I owe you an awful lot," she told him. "My life's changed a great deal since you've been here. And though there's been some tragedies, everything will work out for the best."

"I wish you and Jack a happy life," Lassiter said. "When's the wedding?"

"We'll likely wait until sometime next year, maybe in the spring," she said. "Why don't you come back for it?"

"You never know," Lassiter said.

He mounted his black stallion and turned for the

edge of town. Clara was back with her father and Jack Stanford. They all turned and waved for a long time.

Ahead of him Lassiter saw the sun lowering itself into the mountains. The night would find him at a lonesome creek among the pines, and the next sundown would bring him into a new valley.